THE DAY THE LIGHTS WENT OUT

A SURVIVAL STORY

A NOVEL BY

CALENTHIA YVETTE MILLER

The Day the Lights Went Out:

A Story of Survival ©2025

By Calenthia Yvette Miller

For information, contact:

alurepublishingllc@gmail.com

www.alurepublishing.net

ISBN: 979-89987951-1-4 (Paperback)

Publication Date

DEDICATION

This book is lovingly dedicated to those whose inner light has grown dim due to life's relentless trials and tribulations. During this time, I emphasize the importance of releasing these struggles to the Most High God, recognizing that this journey is far too challenging to undertake alone.

Calenthia

Table of Content

PROLOGUE

The gentle sound of rain softly drummed against the tin roof, creating a soothing melody that filled the cozy interior of Mocha McBride's home. Gradually, Mocha stirred from her sleep as the rhythmic pattern embraced her surroundings. Blinking her bright eyes open, she welcomed the early morning light that seeped into her room. Suddenly, her alarm clock burst to life, filling the air with the uplifting melody of Chaka Khan's "I'm Every Woman."

The energetic anthem reverberated from the ceiling speakers, casting a vibrant tone that danced throughout the space. It urged Mocha to awaken and embrace the day ahead. As the rain continued to fall outside, nurturing the world around her, Mocha could not help but pinch herself, marveling at her surroundings.

A creature of habit, Mocha followed the same rituals every day. After a gentle stretch, she shuffled to the bathroom, where her clothes hung neatly, and her shoes were aligned at the vanity outside her walk-in closet. Following a refreshing shower, she made her way to the kitchen, where the rich aroma of freshly brewed coffee filled the air, setting the perfect tone for the day.

Life was not always this predictable or peaceful.

Let us go back.

THE BEGINNING

CHAPTER 1

BLANK SLATE

Mocha Monroe McBride, a dynamic and accomplished woman in her thirties, had transformed her passion for technology into a thriving software and data analytics business she built from the ground up. Her entrepreneurial journey began in a modest apartment in the heart of the city, filled with second-hand furniture and an unwavering determination to succeed.

Surrounded by a cluttered desk of dual monitors and textbooks on data science, she poured countless hours into developing innovative solutions to complex data problems, often fueled by late-night coffees and the hum of her favorite playlists. Her dedication and resilience shone through in every project, reflecting the vibrant and fulfilling life she had meticulously cultivated for herself.

Yet, beneath the polished veneer of her professional accomplishments, Mocha's life was far from the glamorous narrative often portrayed by success stories. Her early memories were overshadowed by a profound sense of despair and heartache as she navigated a tumultuous childhood, moving from one foster home to another, starting at the tender age of seven and continuing until she aged out of the system at eighteen. Each transition came with its own set of challenges: the anxiety of adjusting to new environments, the fear of forging fleeting relationships, and the relentless yearning for a sense of stability and belonging in a world that felt perpetually chaotic.

Amidst this instability, Mocha often longed for the simple comforts of a nurturing home, where she could lay down roots and build memories. Determined to break the cycle of adversity that marked her early years, she clung to her dreams of a brighter future, fueling her ambition with hopes of higher education, a fulfilling career, and the kind of family bonds she had always desired. Her resilience became her most significant asset, guiding her through the shadows of her past as she worked tirelessly to carve out the life, she envisioned for herself.

With dreams realized and challenges met, she embraced life with vigor, savoring each moment, whether celebrating a hard-earned contract or enjoying quiet evenings with close friends.

Mocha quickly rose to prominence in the business world, becoming one of the youngest Shades of Color Fortune 500 business owners; her company was praised for its innovative contributions to data technology.

That evening, Mocha had just flown in from Seattle, WA, still on cloud nine after receiving an endorsement from the country's largest non-profit, minori-ty-run biochemical and tech firm. This endorsement solidified her commitment to breaking barriers and promoting diversity within the industry, making her a formidable leader and paving the way for greater inclusion and representation in the technology sector.

Once home, Mocha had no plans other than getting food and needed sleep. When Mocha entered her small but rustic home, situated on three acres overlooking a man-made pond, she was still amazed by the serenity each time she looked out through the massive floor-to-ceiling glass door leading to the enclosed lanai.

The room was a vibrant oasis, bursting with lush greenery and exotic blooms from every corner of the globe. Vines cascaded gracefully from hanging baskets, while colorful petals adorned intricate arrangements that filled the air with a sweet, floral fragrance. Mocha glanced out the glass door and watched the sun disappear beyond the distant clouds. Using the remote, she closed the blinds and returned to the kitchen.

Mocha opened the refrigerator door, the cool air spilling out like a gentle breeze. She scanned the shelves lined with food, but nothing caught her eye. The half-empty containers of leftovers seemed uninviting, the wilted greens looked sad, and the colorful fruits lacked any allure. With a sigh, she closed the door, still searching for something to satisfy her hunger. Grabbing her purse and keys, Mocha headed to her favorite spot in town, the Sunset Soul Bistro. Mocha visited the bistro on a business trip to Tennessee a few months ago and was excited to see that it was now in Maryland.

The line extended out the door, filled with a vibrant mix of chatter and laughter as Mocha carefully maneuvered her car into the bustling parking lot. She could see eager patrons glancing at the outdoor menu, their anticipation evident.

Once she stepped inside, the warm ambiance enveloped her, and the host, a cheerful woman with a bright smile, greeted her. With a notepad in hand, the host added Mocha's name to the growing list of diners waiting to enjoy the culinary delights within.

While waiting for her table, Mocha went outside to enjoy the band's sound. The eclectic tones of the steel drums made Mocha sway her hips, reminding her of her time in Jamaica, where the vibrant music was a backdrop to sun-soaked days and carefree nights. This all-inclusive singles retreat had been a thoughtful birthday gift to herself, a chance to break free from her routine and embrace new experiences.

McBride, party of one, came over the intercom. Mocha returned to the bubbly host who had greeted her.

"Hi, Ms. McBride. Fran will escort you to your table."

Fran was a redhead with a thick Irish accent. Her warm demeanor was charming, reminiscent of River Dance, a Broadway performance rooted in traditional Irish music. Fran seated Mocha near the bar. After handing Mocha the menu, Fran shared the day's specials. Mocha opted for the fried catfish and shrimp with fries and a Sprite.

As Mocha surveyed the room, the vibe felt mature and stylish. The potential prospects arrived in various shapes, from tall and muscular to distinguished and intriguing.

As Mocha leisurely sipped her drink, her gaze wandered across the room, filled with the soft hum of conversation and the clinking of glasses. Among the patrons, she noticed a distinguished gentleman sitting alone at the far end of the bar. He exuded an air of quiet confidence, his well-tailored suit accentuating his broad shoulders.

The warm light above him highlighted the silver strands in his hair, contrasting with the deep, rich color of his drink. Mocha could not help but observe the contemplative expression on his face as he methodically stirred his cocktail, seemingly lost in his own world. She could only wonder what thoughts occupied his mind.

Mocha had not been in a relationship for over a year, and she was content with her life, though she occasionally wished for that special someone. Her last relationship had been one-sided and marred by infidelity and verbal abuse. She was still hopeful of finding love again. Fran's arrival with her meal snapped her back to reality.

After finishing dinner, Mocha leaned back, savoring the atmosphere and the sounds of the band. The MC announced a thirty-minute intermission for the band to take a break. Mocha chose to settle the tab and head out. Fran handed her the check and asked that she pay at the bar. Mocha took it to the cashier and returned to the table to give Fran a well-deserved tip.

Mocha's mind replayed the week's wonderful moments as she walked to her car. Just as she reached the parking lot, she realized she had forgotten her favorite scarf, draped casually over the chair where she had been sitting. With a sigh, she turned back and returned to the restaurant, where the host from earlier greeted her with the same bubbly demeanor.

"Excuse me," Mocha said with a polite smile. "I left my...?" Before she could finish her sentence, she noticed it had been neatly placed on the table behind the host. The host handed Mocha the scarf and a glossy postcard advertising the spoken word night, scheduled for next Thursday. She glanced at the card and remembered the first short story she had written at age nine.

The host smiled warmly and said, "You really should come. It's a fantastic opportunity to immerse yourself in the area's incredible talent. You will hear some remarkable performers showcase their skills, and I promise you will not want to miss this wonderful experience."

Mocha looked at the postcard again and considered whether to go. "I will think about it, "she told the host. Before leaving, she glanced to see if the gentleman from earlier was still seated at the bar, and to her dismay, he was not. When she got home, Mocha put her leftovers in the refrigerator and went to her bedroom to unpack her clothes from her trip. She planned to rest this weekend, as she had a busy week ahead of her.

CHAPTER 2

MEMORIES

Over the past month, Mocha has devoted countless hours to an ambitious new project aimed at developing a cutting-edge software solution that addresses key challenges in the technology sector. In this pursuit, she has collaborated closely with Kingston McIntosh, the Chief Financial Officer of Reynolds and Douglas Technology, a firm recognized for its innovative approach to tech development.

As the founder of a Black-owned company led by a woman, Mocha has navigated the complexities of establishing credibility in a predominantly male industry. She has faced this challenge with resilience, leveraging her expertise in software engineering, analytics, and project management, as well as her experience in diverse tech environments.

Mocha has diligently worked to highlight her innovative vision, using detailed presentations and data-driven arguments to counter any biases she encounters. Her commitment to excellence and strategic networking efforts has enabled her to forge valuable connections and gain respect within the sector.

Today, she was focused on finalizing a comprehensive partnership agreement with Reynolds and Douglas Technology, which intricately outlines the terms, responsibilities, and mutual goals of their collaboration. This process has required her to attend numerous meetings, each lasting several hours, during which she discussed in-depth financial projections, resource allocation, and timelines for deliverables. This partnership could establish Radiant Technology and Solutions as a prominent player, and Mocha spared no resources to bring it to fruition.

Mocha reached out to her close friend, Journee Sullivan. They met when they were both sixteen in a group home for girls. The two quickly formed a strong bond, sharing a passion for learning and education. They often spent hours together in the library, reading anything they could find. Although they could have taken a different path, they chose to work hard for what they believed rightfully belonged to them. Their last contact was when they each received scholarships to attend college in different parts of the country.

They reconnected five years ago during a layover in Dallas. Journee has achieved remarkable success over the years. She has been recognized as a powerhouse—a triple threat in Atlanta. Journee earned degrees in psychology, finance, and law, with a specialization in corporate contracts from Stanford. Not only is Journee brilliant and beautiful, but she is also humble. Her unwavering dedication and meticulous attention to detail have been crucial in successfully navigating the intricate complexities of various agreements for Mocha's company. She thoroughly analyzed each aspect to ensure that all stipulations were clearly defined and mutually understood.

Mocha met with Mr. McIntosh and Journee that evening at six to establish a strong foundation for a successful partnership. This groundwork promises to enhance the business capabilities of both parties and create abundant growth opportunities that can be strategically leveraged for long-term success. Mr. McIntosh was impressed with the proposal, but it required the board's approval. He assured Mocha she was a strong candidate for this contract and informed her that she would hear back from him in two weeks with the board's decision.

Mocha escorted Mr. McIntosh out of the conference room while Journee cleared the table and turned off the overhead projector and lights. Just as she was about to close the door, Mocha approached her. “Sis, be honest, do you think I have a chance at getting this contract?” Journee shrugged her shoulders. “I’m good at reading people’s body language, but Mr. McIntosh was difficult to decipher.” “Thank you for flying in and for all your help. As always, you did an amazing job!” Mocha said. “You’re welcome, but girl, when will you invest in a larger space?” I could smell the mint on Mr. McIntosh’s breath.” Journee and Mocha laughed as they walked to the elevator together.

Mocha ran the business from a charming loft in the bustling Melford Towne Center. This welcoming space, adorned with colorful artwork and warm lighting, was ideally located just steps away from various restaurants, retail and grocery stores, art galleries, and a bookstore. It offered easy access to the freeway, making it an ideal hub for creativity and convenience. The greatest advantage, however, was the affordable rent, which allowed Mocha to invest more in her business without the burden of high overhead costs. Additionally, it was just a short distance away from her home.

Mocha and Journee enjoyed a late dinner at a cozy Italian restaurant just a block from her office. The warm ambiance provided the perfect setting for their final moments before Journee’s departure. They savored the rich, handmade pasta paired with bold red wine, sharing laughter and stories that lingered in the air, much like the delicious aroma of garlic and herbs.

After their meal, Mocha drove Journee to her hotel, the city lights illuminating the darkness as they navigated the bustling streets. Journee was set to take a red-eye flight to Spain, a long-awaited adventure they had been planning for over a year, filled with dreams of exploring Barcelona’s vibrant culture and breathtaking countryside landscapes.

Mocha had initially planned to join Journee on this trip; however, she ultimately made the tough decision to cancel after talks of a potential contract with Reynolds and Douglas Technology, as well as several other high-profile clients, that could significantly advance her career.

Balancing professional commitments and personal aspirations was never easy, but the weight of these contracts was too significant to ignore. As they approached the hotel, the bittersweet feeling of goodbyes hung in the air, but their friendship remained strong, promising future adventures together. And this is why Mocha cherished Journee, as she was one of the positive reminders of her childhood.

The next day, Mocha woke to the soft, golden light streaming through her curtains. However, the remnants of the previous night's indulgence weighed heavily on her. The extra bottles of rich, velvety Moscato wine had not only clouded her thoughts but also conspired to keep her nestled deep in her inviting goose-down comforter. As she lay there, the familiar scent of brewed coffee drifting in from the kitchen made it even more tempting to linger in bed. Mocha closed her eyes and drifted back to sleep.

It was midday when Mocha finally got out of bed. After showering, she went to the kitchen to brew a cup of coffee with four sugars and two French vanilla creamers. Stirring her coffee into a beautiful caramel hue, she toasted two slices of cinnamon raisin bread and sat at the table, watching nature through her window.

Lost in thought about her life, Mocha had been considering the possibility of searching for her biological family for the past three years. It was not until last week that she discovered a storage box containing her early writings while cleaning her garage. Then she remembered the host mentioning Thursday's spoken word night at the Bistro. She walked to her home office and retrieved several spiral notebooks filled with her writings.

As she read, she was struck by how creative she had been at such an early age. Mocha noticed what appeared to be tear stains on the left side of the pages. Even after all these years, she still felt the pain of uncertainty. One of her writings made her marvel at her strength, but it also raised questions about why she had been placed in foster care. This entry was written when Mocha was a teenager, just a few weeks before she was officially released from foster care.

Ignite the Fire Within

My inner light has not merely flickered timidly in the shadows; there have been remarkable moments when it has shone with intensity, illuminating the darkness that often feels overwhelming and oppressive. During these times, I have felt a sense of empowerment, as if my essence could push back against despair and uncertainty. I have come to realize how easily doubt can seep into my thoughts, casting a veil over clarity and making every decision seem fraught with ambiguity. The struggle against this doubt is a constant battle, reminding me of the fragility of confidence and the strength of perseverance. Yet, when my light shone, it brought clarity and enveloped me like a warm embrace, reassuring me that I was not alone and that brighter days were possible.

Today, I am isolating myself to protect my peace. And before you ask, I am not running away or hiding; I am building the strength to keep going in this race.

Memories of her younger years echoed vividly, like a cherished old photograph. She could remember, as far back as three or four years old, dressed in a floral-printed jumper. Her sandy brown hair was tied neatly into two playful ponytails, each adorned with bright, colorful ribbons. In her mind's eye, she could see herself standing on the weathered wooden porch of her childhood home, its paint peeling slightly from years of sun exposure.

She gazed up at an older woman, perhaps a grandmother with warm eyes a gentle smile, and silver-streaked hair, as she asked with innocent curiosity when she would be allowed to ride her tricycle. Mocha recalled the tricycle in vivid detail: it was a blend of white and red, with a shiny chrome bell on the handlebar that jingled softly as she pedaled and a small woven basket attached to the center bar, perfect for carrying her favorite toys. Each detail was etched in her memory, a testament to the joy and innocence of her early childhood.

At the age of seven, everything changed. The sweet, carefree memories of childhood innocence quickly faded as Mocha found herself in her first foster home with Bettie Jo Engels. Mrs. Engels had two biological children and a parade of foster kids, ranging from six months to ten years old, each with their own needs and stories.

The first few months were quiet, allowing Mocha to adjust to her new surroundings. By the time one year had passed, the weight of responsibility rested heavily on her shoulders as she cared for the two youngest children, changing diapers, calming tears, and sharing her meager meals. Many nights, her stomach growled with hunger, as she often had little more than a few scraps to eat after she fed the other children her meal.

Mocha's school attendance dropped alarmingly as she struggled to balance her new responsibilities with her education. The truancy officer and social worker soon arrived at the house unannounced. Upon entering the front door, the social worker quickly assessed the dire conditions of the home. The reality of neglect was evident, leading to the prompt and necessary decision to remove all the children from Mrs. Engels' care.

The cycle of moving from one home to another became routine for Mocha. She never felt comfortable, so she stored her few clothes in garbage bags and her backpack, knowing she could be taken at any moment. This thrusts Mocha into the uncertainty of yet another chapter in her young life.

Mocha removed the final entry from the notebook and gently returned it to the storage box. This marked the beginning of her commitment to uncovering the truth about her biological family's origins.

CHAPTER 3

BREATHE

As the workday drew to a close, Mocha sank deeper into her chair, feeling utterly exhausted. The minutes of the day lingered in her mind after she had just finished a lengthy Zoom meeting with her management team. The screen displayed familiar faces, each representing a crucial pillar of the company.

Justyn, the meticulous lead data scientist, shared insightful analytics that guided their strategic decisions. Sloane, the senior software engineer, presented an impressive overview of the latest development progress, highlighting the sleek interface her team had tirelessly refined. Hudson, who oversees software design, engaged the group with his visionary ideas for enhancing user experience. Greer, the sharp-eyed cybersecurity expert, raised important points about safeguarding their systems against increasing threats. River and Emerald, the duo leading the programming and network architecture aspects, demonstrated their usual constructive collaboration, discussing optimizations that could advance their projects.

After navigating technical challenges and brainstorming innovative solutions, Harlan Mocha's executive secretary announced she would send out the meeting minutes by the end of the week. Mocha felt the weight of the day's intensity settle over her, yearning for a moment of respite before tackling tomorrow's tasks. As she gathered her belongings, her phone buzzed. It was Journee; she had only briefly spoken to her since returning from Spain.

"Hey, sis, how are you? "Mocha took a deep breath and said, exhausted. It has been an exceptionally long day. "Are you on your way home?" Journee asked. Yes, Mocha replied.

Mocha asked Journee about her recent trip to Spain, during which Mocha revealed her intention to begin searching for her family. Journee, as always, expressed her support and offered to help Mocha. However, when Mocha proposed that they embark on the search together, Journee declined for unspecified reasons. Respecting Journee's decision, Mocha chose not to press the issue, acknowledging that everyone has the right to decide when to engage in such personal processes.

"Have you heard from Mr. McIntosh?" "No, not yet," Mocha replied. Thursday will mark two weeks. I will give him until the end of the week. If he hasn't called by then, I'll reach out to check the status."

Mocha ended her call with Journee as she pulled into the driveway. She had intentionally chosen this area while searching for a new place to live, drawn to its seclusion and the perfect blend of country and city vibes. Towering trees lined the street, creating a tranquil atmosphere far removed from the hustle and bustle of urban life.

Her commute to the office was a manageable twenty-five minutes, allowing her to enjoy both the tranquility of her surroundings and the convenience of urban amenities. As she exited her car, she glanced at the vast acreage she had purchased, contemplating its possibilities. The idea of adding a few charming tiny homes began to take shape in her mind. She imagined them as cozy retreats for weekend getaways or vacation rentals, which could provide a promising source of passive income to enhance her lifestyle. The vision excited her, filling her with a sense of purpose and anticipation for the future.

As Mocha opened the mailbox and retrieved the documents inside, she glanced up at the sound of a passing car honking while reviewing the mail in her hand. Her neighbor, Maxwell, had moved into the house three doors down a few months earlier. Mocha met Maxwell when a package was mistakenly delivered to her address. The way he laughed at the mix-up, his warm smile putting her at ease, left a lasting impression on her. However, it did not prevent her from letting her guard down.

After parking her car in the garage and stepping into the mudroom, Mocha kicked off her shoes and headed to the kitchen, where she placed the mail on the island. Not feeling particularly hungry, she washed her hands and made a turkey and cheese sandwich on potato bread, grabbed a bag of salt-and-vinegar kettle chips, and drank a bottle of water while sorting through the pile of mail. As usual, there was more junk than anything else. However, one piece of mail caught her eye: from Spelman College, her alma mater. She opened the letter and was surprised to hear from them, as it had been over twelve years since her graduation.

The dean of students' letter inquired whether Mocha would be interested in serving as a panelist at the Data Science Round-Up. The forum features prominent leaders in the technology field who answer questions from students entering the profession. Mocha felt honored to be invited and regarded as a leader in the industry, especially coming from Spelman. The deadline to respond to the invitation was not until August, so there was plenty of time to decide whether she would accept. After clearing the island and disposing of unwanted mail, an empty water bottle, and a paper plate, Mocha settled onto the couch to watch television.

The floodlights illuminated, signaling that someone was approaching the house. Mocha stood up from the sofa and walked over to the surveillance system she had installed shortly after closing on the house. The sun's glare made it impossible to see the figure walking up the driveway. Mocha switched to the camera facing the door and saw it was Maxwell. Dressed in a tailored navy suit that highlighted his athletic build, he exuded an effortless charm, his mouth turning into a disarming smile at the corners.

Speaking through the ring camera, Mocha greeted him. Hi neighbor. I received another letter from you that was delivered to me again. Unlocking the door, Maxwell handed the mail to her. Maxwell remarked, "You would think that after living here for over twelve months, the postman would know where we live."

"Yeah, you'd think so," Mocha replied. "I guess Mocha could be confused with Maxwell, but that's unlikely," she said, laughing. "It would definitely be an oversight on their part since I'm not as beautiful as you are," Maxwell said. Mocha began to blush but kept her guard up. "Thanks for your kind words. It's getting late, and I have a busy day ahead of me tomorrow. Again, I appreciate you bringing the mail to me."

Mocha shut the door and watched the surveillance camera as Maxwell walked down the driveway to his sleek black sports car. As he approached his vehicle, she could not shake the feeling that beneath his polished exterior lay a hint of something darker, just waiting for the right moment to emerge. This left her spirit unsettled. Mocha finished watching the news, showered, and headed to bed.

Mocha awoke feeling exhausted after a restless night. Her mind would not settle, and she had several meetings scheduled for the day, including one with a private detective she had hired to begin her search for her family. She felt both excited and nervous about uncovering the missing answers to a life she desperately needed to explore.

During the night, Mocha sifted through the box of her writings and found a photo of a young girl she believed to be herself. However, after examining it again, she realized it was not. Her mind was now overloaded, and she wondered who this girl could be. Was it perhaps her mother or sister? Mocha flipped the photo over to see if there were any distinctive markings; there were none. She placed the photo in her backpack and planned to show it to the private detective when they met later that day.

Mocha arrived at the office just before seven. She thoughtfully ordered breakfast for the team, which included fresh croissants, hearty breakfast burritos, assorted bagels with cream cheese, and a variety of beverages, such as freshly squeezed orange juice, coffee, and smoothies. Her team deserved this; it was the least she could do for their hard work in making the company successful.

Harlan arrived at the office first and greeted Mocha with a warm "Good morning" and a sincere "Thank you." Soon, the other team members gathered in the break room to join in the festivities. Mocha took pride in the work culture she had cultivated- a culture filled with love and admiration for one another, something she had missed during her upbringing. Harlan reminded Mocha about her meeting with Montana McGee at ten. Her friend Loren, who worked for a well-known lawyer in Tennessee, had highly recommended him. Loren noted that Montana was thorough and easy on the eyes. Mocha chuckled as she considered that if she worked with him for an undisclosed amount of time, at least he was handsome.

In the days leading up to their first meeting, Montana emailed Mocha, asking thoughtful questions to gather crucial information for the case. These inquiries covered everything from details about Mocha's family history to potential leads that might help track them down. As Mocha reflected on the questions, she realized she had some gaps in her knowledge, which heightened her determination to uncover the truth about her family's whereabouts.

Harlan knocked on Mocha's door to inform her that Mr. McGee was in the conference room. Mocha checked her appearance in the mirror before entering. Mr. McGee stood up when Mocha walked in. He extended his hand and said, "It is a pleasure to meet you, Mrs. McBride."

"Thank you for taking my case, Mr. McGee. I've heard great things about you."

"Well, I hope to meet all your expectations." " If we are to work together, please call me Montana. " Duly noted. Please call me Mocha."

Mocha's meeting with Montana lasted over two hours. She provided him with as much information as possible, though it wasn't much. She also gave him the photo she had found. Before concluding their meeting, he asked if she could send him a copy of her birth certificate and the name of her last placement in foster care. He emphasized that such cases can be lengthy and take a toll on individuals. Mocha agreed with his assertion that it had already been stressful, but she also admitted that Loren was right; he was easy on the eyes.

Chapter 4

SHADED

Today marks three weeks since Kingston McIntosh's anticipated deadline for responding to their potential collaboration. Despite Mocha's relentless efforts to reach him—she called and left multiple messages on both his direct line and email—there has still been no response.

Mocha was known for not letting any grass grow under her feet. She has scheduled an important meeting with Solar Technology for next Thursday at 10 AM. The owner, an innovative entrepreneur acclaimed for his work in renewable energy solutions, expressed eagerness to discuss a promising project that Solar Technology is developing in partnership with the Institute of Agronomics.

This project seeks to integrate solar energy solutions into modern farming techniques, potentially revolutionizing agricultural practices and enhancing sustainability. This type of venture is new for Mocha, but she remains optimistic that this meeting could unlock new avenues for collaboration and funding opportunities.

The day was winding down, and Mocha had no plans for the evening, not wanting to go home. Instead, she chose to visit the bistro. The parking lot was packed, forcing Mocha to park in the overflow section. Inside, it buzzed with people, leaving only standing room. The host, a cheerful presence amidst the chaos, informed her that there would be a one-hour wait. With her name added to the list, Mocha immersed herself in the lively atmosphere as the same talented band from her last visit played again, their melodies blending with the sounds of conversation and laughter, creating the perfect backdrop she craved after such a hectic week.

An announcement echoed over the PA system, calling solo diners to the reservation podium. Mocha made her way over as the host explained that, due to the large crowd, guests were being asked if they would mind joining a party of four. Mocha agreed, and the host waited for the other guests to approach the podium. The waiter then escorted them to the table. Mocha noticed only two people were seated at the table, so she assumed the other guests had chosen not to join them. Their waiter—a tall man with dark hair and a friendly demeanor—introduced himself as Bryson and took their orders effortlessly, suggesting a few popular dishes.

The conversation around the table quickly became animated as everyone introduced themselves. Mocha learned that Morgan, a freelance graphic designer and journalist with an adventurous spirit, frequently traveled to remote locations to gather her stories. Meanwhile, Lance, the easygoing economics professor, shared intriguing insights into global economic trends.

Just as Mocha was about to place her belongings in the empty seat, Bryson approached the table with the fourth guest. To her surprise, the man seated across from her was none other than the gentleman she had spotted at the bar over a month earlier. Just before taking his seat, he introduced himself with a friendly smile. "Jaxzon Jeffries." Mocha noticed an accent but could not quite place it. Now, she found herself staring, almost starstruck. Determined not to appear thirsty or desperate, Mocha shifted her focus to the menu and waited for Morgan and Lance to introduce themselves.

"I didn't catch your name," he said. His smooth, baritone voice made her sit up and take notice. "My name is Mocha," she replied. "It's a pleasure to be dining with all of you tonight," Jaxzon said. "It's crowded tonight," Morgan commented. "I've never seen the restaurant this packed," Lance added.

Bryson returned with drinks and appetizers, and Morgan inquired about the crowd. Bryson replied, "Every second Thursday of the month features spoken word." Mocha remembered the postcard she had received the previous month, promoting the event. Bryson mentioned that the program would take place on the enclosed patio outside. Mocha rummaged through her purse and found the letter she had come across a few weeks earlier in the storage box. She glanced at the words before quickly putting the letter back in her purse. Bryson collected everyone's dinner selections and headed to the kitchen to place the order.

"So, Mocha, what do you do for a living?" Jaxzon asked, his deep voice rich and resonant, each word tinged with a captivating accent. Mocha paused, caught off guard by the unexpected question. It wasn't that she lacked a ready answer; rather, the slow cadence of his speech had momentarily thrown her off balance, diverting her attention from her own thoughts.

After a brief moment of hesitation, she shook off her surprise and composed herself, her mind racing to formulate a coherent response. The air around them felt charged with an awkward silence, heavy with unspoken expectations. Sensing the tension, Morgan quickly interjected with a warm comment about Jaxzon's distinctive accent, which lightened the atmosphere and brought a smile to Mocha's face, easing her nerves and inviting her back into the conversation.

Now that Mocha had shared her profession, Morgan turned to Jaxzon and asked what he did for a living. Just as Jaxzon was about to respond, his phone buzzed. He excused himself politely from the table, moving fluidly and confidently. This brief distraction allowed Mocha to admire how he carried himself as he walked away. It had been far too long since she had encountered such a captivating figure; his broad shoulders and natural charm instantly captivated her, stirring a quiet admiration within her that lingered long after he had vanished from sight.

After taking his call, Jaxzon walked back to the table, where steaming plates of entrées awaited everyone. The rich scents of roasted vegetables, savory meats, and fragrant spices filled the air, tantalizing their senses. Before they dove into the feast, Jaxzon requested a moment of blessing for the food. With his eyes closed and hands clasped, he delivered a heartfelt prayer that flowed like poetry, causing the laughter and chatter around the table to fade to a hush in Mocha's ears, allowing her to absorb the moment fully. It was a beautiful reminder of gratitude and togetherness before they savored each delicious bite.

The conversation resumed as everyone became more engaged in the discussed topics. Morgan asked Jaxzon again what he did for a living, and Jaxzon replied that he was a marketing executive. Mocha felt curious and wanted to learn more about his occupation but chose not to pursue it. Dinner concluded when Bryson asked if anyone wanted dessert before distributing the checks. As Mocha placed her credit card in the billfold, she overheard one of the patrons complimenting Jaxzon on his looks and speculating whether he was single. Quietly in her mind, Mocha wondered the same thing.

She watched as many patrons began to leave the restaurant and head toward the enclosed patio to listen to the spoken word contestants. Bryson handed Mocha her credit card, without the receipt, for her to sign. Noticing her puzzled expression, he explained that Jaxzon had taken care of it. Not wanting to draw attention to him, she gathered her belongings. Before leaving, she said goodbye to Morgan, Lance, and Jaxzon, thanking them for their engaging conversation over dinner.

Jaxzon asked if she would stay for the show, and Mocha politely declined. After several minutes of back-and-forth chatter, they persuaded Mocha to stay, and she was glad she did. The raw talent displayed by each performer was transformative and enlightening. One performance reduced Mocha to tears as he spoke of abandonment and yearning for a life beyond his reach. Overwhelmed by a sudden rush of emotion, Mocha felt it was time to leave. Gathering her belongings, she excused herself from the table and left the venue.

As Mocha approached her vehicle, she heard her name being called. It was Morgan. "Hey, are you okay?' Not wanting to appear as an emotional wreck, Mocha sighed heavily and replied, "Yes, it's been a long day, and I have a lot on my mind. I genuinely hope this won't be the last time we see each other." Her voice carried a hint of vulnerability, revealing the weight of her thoughts.

Morgan smiled softly in response, her eyes conveying a shared sentiment, as she replied, "I hope not."

As she opened the car door, Morgan slipped a business card into Mocha's hand and exchanged a warm goodnight. Mocha sat in her vehicle, her mind swirling with unresolved questions and lingering emotions. The soft hum of the engine contrasted starkly with the chaos of her thoughts as she stared absently out the window.

A firm tap on the passenger window suddenly jolted her back to reality. Startled, she turned to find Jaxzon standing there, his brow furrowed in concern. His anxious demeanor made her heart race. Jaxzon raised his hand, gesturing for her to roll down the window. With a deliberate motion, she lowered the glass, bracing herself for whatever was on his mind.

IDENTITY

Chapter 5

OUT OF SIGHT

Today marks a year since Maxwell returned to Maryland, and what a year it has been. He has settled into a charming rental just on the outskirts of the city, a place that feels like home with its warm hues and inviting atmosphere. His job has flourished, providing him with both fulfillment and a sense of stability. However, the highlight of his new life is his neighbor, Mocha, who is absolutely stunning!

Soon after moving to the neighborhood, he first caught sight of her from a distance. Her presence was captivating as she tended her garden, planting vibrant flowers near her mailbox. The way her sweatpants hugged her curves was undeniably intoxicating, leaving a lasting impression that added a spark to his everyday life.

***

When Maxwell's boss, a no-nonsense manager known for her high expectations and relentless drive, approached him with a proposal to lead an ambitious new project in Maryland, he felt a wave of reluctance wash over him. The prospect of a career-defining opportunity should have thrilled him, but instead, anxiety gnawed at his insides.

Maxwell had grown accustomed to the comfortable routine of his modest high-rise apartment, nestled in the vibrant heart of Culver City, California. Sunlight filtered through the large windows each morning, casting a warm glow on the walls decorated with art from local artists, which stood in stark contrast to the tumultuous feelings brewing inside him.

***

As memories flooded back to the small town of Maplewood, where he had grown up, he felt a tug at his heart. Maplewood was a nostalgic landscape of shaded streets and familiar faces—a place where every sidewalk seemed paved with pivotal events from his youth. Yet, it was also a town steeped in pain; it was where he encountered heartbreak, loss, and the harsh reality of his family's struggles. Each corner resonated with laughter and tears, making the thought daunting and unsettling.

His mind raced as he weighed the professional opportunity—an impressive promotion that could elevate his career—against the heavy emotional baggage tied to that location. The decision hung heavily in the air, laden with the weight of his past and the pressure of expectation.

Maxwell found himself grappling with conflicting desires: the ambition to soar professionally and the need to confront his past. He could no longer run from or hide behind the shadows of his childhood; at this juncture, he needed to face them head-on, seeking closure and possibly even peace in a place that had once shaped him.

Before leaving California, he openly shared his feelings about the upcoming move with his therapist, Dr. Patel. The cozy room, adorned with calming artwork and the faint scent of lavender, provided the perfect backdrop for such a vulnerable conversation. Dr. Patel listened attentively, validating his concerns about leaving behind familiar surroundings and cherished friendships.

With a warm and reassuring tone, Dr. Patel encouraged him to seek counseling in his new city, emphasizing the importance of continuity in his healing journey. She reminded him that while the prospect of change can be daunting, it often catalyzes personal growth and discovery. Her words resonated with him, planting a seed of hope that he could navigate this transition and emerge even stronger on the other side.

Maxwell recognized the importance of this advice; he didn't want to stagnate or regress. He firmly believed that speaking with someone who couldn't fully relate to his unique experiences and struggles was a waste of his financial resources and emotional energy. This realization marked a pivotal moment for him as he sought someone who could truly understand the complexities of his life. He also understood that he needed to stay focused and avoid any triggers that could lead to a relapse.

He had not revisited his old neighborhood, a place filled with cherished yet painful memories, and he was uncertain whether he would ever feel ready to do so. The streets resonated with youth and familiarity but also with unresolved trauma. Still having not found a therapist to his liking, Maxwell opted to use meditation and routine workouts as a form of therapy, which, for now, worked. Occasionally, he would schedule telemedicine appointments with Dr. Patel, but soon, that would no longer be an option as she was moving out of the country.

Maxwell stepped into the warm spray of the shower, letting the water wash away the remnants of sleep. As he lathered his body with fragrant body wash, he couldn't shake the anticipation brewing in his stomach. Today was significant—he would meet with Tristan Long, the regional operational director who oversaw the bustling offices in Chicago, Indianapolis, and Cleveland. Maxwell had spent weeks preparing for this meeting, meticulously reviewing reports and strategizing his presentation. He had heard that Tristan was a hard nut to crack and needed to bring his A-game.

He towel-dried and glanced at the clock, aware that every minute counted. This was an opportunity to impress Tristan and showcase his vision for optimizing operations across the key regions. With a focused mindset, he dressed in a crisp, charcoal-gray suit and polished his shoes, feeling a surge of confidence. Today wasn't just another day at the office; it was the chance to make his move.

Once dressed, Maxwell prepared a protein shake, grabbed his satchel bag, and headed to his car. The soft, golden light of the early morning sun filtered through the scattered clouds, casting a warm glow over the tree-lined street.

As he drove past Mocha's house, his mind wandered. He envisioned her infectious laugh and how her eyes sparkled like stars when they shared a story, making even the dullest days brighter. He wondered whether she was getting ready for work or curled under her soft, warm blankets, savoring the last moments of peaceful sleep.

He had a fondness for her. Yet, the thrill of his feelings was accompanied by a hint of anxiety; he understood the importance of caution and felt that patience was essential. He resolved to wait for the perfect moment, one that would signal the right time to ask her out.

CHAPTER 6

UNEXPECTED

Mocha stood in her office, gazing out the expansive floor-to-ceiling window that offered a panoramic view of the bustling city below. Her thoughts swirled like the clouds in the sky, reflecting her current state of uncertainty. Earlier that day, the highly anticipated meeting with Solar Technology to discuss a potential partnership had been unexpectedly canceled. The receptionist had assured her that the lead executive at Solar Technology would reach out to reschedule. Still, as the hours passed without any communication, Mocha felt a growing sense of impatience.

Taking a deep breath, she recognized the urgent need to refocus her efforts and actively explore alternative markets that could offer new opportunities for her company's growth and expansion. However, she also understood that the last-minute cancellation of today's meeting with the potential client, while disappointing, was not the root cause of her inattentiveness; it was Jaxzon.

It had been two weeks since Mocha last saw Jaxzon in the bistro's parking lot. She was immediately taken aback when she turned and saw Jaxzon at the passenger window. The concern in his mysterious eyes left her puzzled and slightly breathless. She could sense an unspoken tension in the air, causing her heart to race as she tried to decipher what was happening in his mind.

Jaxzon gestured for her to roll down the window. As the window slowly inched down, Mocha felt nervous; her heart raced, and her stomach tightened—an anxious sensation that often left her momentarily mute whenever he spoke. The cool breeze rushed in, carrying the intoxicating scent of nectarine blossom and honey, but all she could focus on was the intensity of his gaze, which left her breathless and apprehensive.

The warm, soothing tones of Jaxzon's voice filled the interior of Mocha's car, creating an intimate cocoon that seemed to shield them from the world outside. "Is everything okay? Why are you sad?" His words, imbued with genuine concern, wrapped around her like a soft blanket. Mocha found herself captivated, unable to look away as she took in the sincerity etched in his eyes. The weight of his question hung in the air, prompting her to close her eyes and savor the moment—a delicate blend of vulnerability and comfort that stirred something deep within her.

Jaxzon gently brushed his fingers against Mocha's forearm, prompting her to blink awake. Startled by his unexpected touch, she shifted slightly in her seat, her heart racing. He settled beside her in the car, his gaze unwavering and filled with concern. "Do I need to call for some medical assistance?" Jaxzon asked, his voice laced with genuine worry. "No, I am fine. It has been an exceptionally long day and week. I need to go home and get some rest." Hesitantly, Jaxzon agreed to let Mocha drive home as he insisted on her getting a taxi.

Mocha didn't want Jaxzon to worry about her, so she agreed to sit and talk until he felt at ease. They engaged in a conversation that flowed effortlessly, discussing a wide range of topics. Jaxzon shared snippets of his life—his passion for reading, which spanned genres from classic literature to contemporary thrillers; his journey as a self-taught guitar player who diligently practiced in his small apartment; and his talent for playing the jazz saxophone, where his soulful melodies often filled the evening air. Each revelation painted a richer picture of who he was, deepening her fascination with him.

Realizing the hour was growing late and with only two vehicles remaining in the dimly lit bistro parking lot, Jaxzon glanced at his watch and sighed. He reluctantly pulled out his phone to call for his ride. As he waited, the bistro's gentle hum of conversation and light music faded into the background. The glow from the overhead lights cast a warm ambiance, wrapping around them like a soft embrace.

When his driver arrived, Jaxzon turned to Mocha with a sincere smile. "Thank you for such a delightful evening," he said, his eyes reflecting the warmth of their shared moments. He hesitated momentarily before adding, "Please call me once you get home. I'd love to know you made it safe."

Mocha nodded, her heart fluttering with a mix of happiness and melancholy. After bidding Jaxzon good night, she sat there, her thoughts swirling. The night had been filled with laughter and sparkles of connection, and now, the cool night air felt heavy with the weight of parting. She felt an unexpected pang of longing, wishing this enchanting evening could stretch on just a little longer.

CHAPTER 7

FULFILLMENT

Jaxzon Jeffries arrived at Baltimore-Washington International Airport on Saturday evening. After checking into his Airbnb, he took a shower and napped, tired from his flight from Madagascar. Following his rejuvenating sleep, Jaxzon reviewed the places he planned to visit in Washington, DC, Maryland, and Virginia.

This trip was overdue and well-deserved. Many of his friends suggested dining at the harbor and trying the Maryland Blue Crab, which is known for its sweet, tender meat. They recommended The Food Market; a trendy restaurant celebrated for its creative twists on classic dishes. Jaxzon also noted the Capitol on his itinerary, excited to explore its rich history and discover the numerous exhibits and museums that showcase the nation's past.

On Sunday, Jaxzon visited the National Museum of African American History and Culture in Washington, D.C. The museum, which spans ten floors, showcases the rich and diverse history of the many African Americans who have made significant contributions to shaping this nation. Jaxzon knew this would be one of the first places he explored as someone of mixed heritage. He wanted to immerse himself in as much history as possible. When he reached the fifth floor, the guide indicated that the museum would close soon. After confirming the operating hours for the week, Jaxzon planned to return and complete his tour.

***

During his formative years in Germany, Jaxzon embraced his identity as a person of Afro-German descent. The multicultural environment of his hometown, Cologne, provided diversity, but he learned very little about African American history in the classroom, which left him feeling disconnected from a heritage he yearned to explore. Despite his parents' efforts to bridge this gap through stories and discussions at home, it wasn't quite the same as learning about it in an educational setting.

Jaxzon's early memories include a remarkable trip to the United States with his parents when he was a child. This adventure was both exciting and touching, as it allowed him to connect with his father's extended family, who warmly embraced him, sharing stories, traditions, and a deep sense of belonging that he had yet to experience fully.

At seventeen, Jaxzon revisited the States, this time with a more purposeful intention as he embarked on a tour of prominent colleges and universities. He was particularly drawn to Fisk University, renowned for its rich history and vibrant cultural atmosphere, as well as Grambling State University, celebrated for its strong sense of community and academic excellence. However, his aspirations for higher education in the States faced significant obstacles when unexpected family dynamics and financial constraints arose, forcing him to put his dreams on hold. This setback left him reflecting on his journey and the paths yet to explore as he sought to carve out his own identity amid the complexities of his background.

Driven by a deep desire to reconnect with his cultural heritage, Jaxzon eagerly embraced the opportunity to work alongside Donovan Singleton, a devoted missionary known for his transformative contributions to communities. During his senior year at the University of Cologne, he traveled to the stunning city of Cape Town, South Africa, where the iconic Table Mountain towers over vibrant neighborhoods.

Immersed in the city's dynamic atmosphere, Jaxzon engaged in various outreach programs designed to uplift and empower local residents. He spent time at schools, inspiring eager students with creative workshops, and he worked with Donovan to provide essential resources to underserved families, ensuring they had access to education and basic necessities.

Additionally, Jaxzon participated in cultural exchange initiatives that celebrated the rich tapestry of South African history and traditions. Through meaningful thoughtful conversations with local community members, he gained invaluable insights into their struggles and triumphs, deepening his understanding of both his own identity and the powerful connections that transcend borders. This transformative experience not only enriched Jaxzon's appreciation for his roots but also sparked a lasting passion for making a positive impact in the lives of others.

After earning a degree in civil engineering and a minor in air quality and solid waste management, Jaxzon embarked on a seven-year journey that spanned an expansive period. His travels took him across diverse landscapes, from bustling cities to remote villages, as he engaged in heartfelt missionary work focused on sustainable development and community empowerment.

He collaborated with local artisans and engineers, helping to construct critical infrastructure that improved living conditions and fostered environmental awareness in often overlooked communities. Ultimately, Jaxzon settled on the idyllic Caribbean Island of Grenada, renowned for its breathtaking beaches, vibrant culture, and rich biodiversity.

Here, he took on a role as a civil engineer and government contractor, contributing to projects that revitalized public spaces and enhanced essential services. While the financial rewards were commendable, the routine nature of the work left him yearning for deeper fulfillment and a more significant impact on the world around him.

Driven by a lifelong passion for gardening that had flourished during his travels, Jaxzon resolved to intertwine his engineering skills with his love for the earth. He envisioned a venture that would sustain him financially and foster community connections through urban gardening initiatives. With a commitment to environmental stewardship, he aimed to educate locals about sustainable practices, bringing life and hope to urban spaces while inspiring others to appreciate the beauty and utility of nature. This new path was not just about planting seeds in the soil; it was about sowing resilience and nurturing community bonds.

Inspired by his vision, Jaxzon reached out to his good friend and mentor, Donovan. Recognizing Jaxzon's passion for environmental conservation, Donovan encouraged him to apply for a grant dedicated to this vital cause. Although it seemed like a long shot, Jaxzon poured his heart into the application process, and after an agonizing three-year wait, he received the incredible news: he had been awarded a $220,000 grant. This substantial funding became the seed capital for his ambitious project. However, the journey was far from easy, as it took another five years of dedication and hard work before he finally began to see a return on his investment.

At forty-one, Jaxzon stands at the crossroads of achievement and simplicity, appreciating the fruits of his labor. He has accumulated a modest fortune yet embraces a low-maintenance lifestyle that reflects his values. His comfortable ranch home, with three cozy bedrooms, exudes warmth and tranquility, surrounded by the gentle embrace of nature. Parked in the driveway is his reliable four-door 2017 Honda Accord Sedan, a symbol of practicality and understated elegance, perfectly complementing his unpretentious way of life. Much of his wealth is donated to charities, including orphanages and the construction of schools and hospitals, while ensuring that his family is well taken care of.

Jaxzon made a heartfelt promise to his parents, who were now gracefully navigating their late sixties, to visit his relatives on his father's side during his stay in the United States. True to his word, he meticulously arranged for his secretary to carve out time in his busy itinerary for a journey to the charming and historic Princess Anne County, Virginia, where his family roots lay deep.

Although his memories of his father's relatives were foggy and distant, fragments of joyful family gatherings occasionally flickered in his mind—laughter echoing through sun-drenched rooms and the aroma of home-cooked meals wafting in the air.

His father often reminisced about their lively reunions, sharing stories that painted vibrant pictures of the family's rich history, filled with warmth and camaraderie. Jaxzon couldn't recall the faces of his aunts and uncles clearly, but he remembered the sound of their voices and the sense of connection that came with their shared heritage. It had been years since he last saw them when he was seven or eight, but he longed to forge those bonds anew.

As he contemplated the journey ahead, Jaxzon felt a mix of anticipation and a sense of nostalgia. He hoped this trip would enrich his understanding of his roots and create vivid new memories to add to the tapestry of his past, enabling him to rediscover the essence of the family he had been apart from for so long.

CHAPTER 8

UNCERTAINTY

Mocha had just hung up the phone after a lengthy conversation with Montana. Their discussion revolved around the birth certificate that Montana had received. Montana still had several pressing questions that needed clarification, particularly about the discrepancies he noticed in the dates and names listed. The echo of Montana's voice lingered in her mind, and with a furrowed brow, she contemplated the implications of these inconsistencies as she prepared to redial Montana's number.

The uncertainty Mocha felt was as though she were reliving a nightmare. An icy grip washed over her, reminiscent of that haunting day she first walked through the door of fifteen fifty-five Carvel Court. She could almost hear the echoes of her hesitant footsteps as she entered the sterile, unfamiliar environment, where the walls were painted a dull gray, and the air was thick with the scent of turpentine. Memories flooded back—the anxiety knotting her stomach, the tear-stained cheeks, and the sense of dislocation that accompanied the strangers meant to offer her a new home. At that moment, the emotional turmoil felt strikingly similar, leaving her with a heavy weight of doubt and fear about the future.

Mocha fought to suppress her tears and simmering anger, but the emotions surged within her, too powerful to contain. With a shaky breath, she buried her face in the delicate palms of her petite hands, allowing the floodgates to open as she cried uncontrollably. The sting of yet another disappointment felt like an unbearable weight on her chest; she couldn't face it again, especially not now.

Gathering her scattered belongings, she informed Harlan of her decision to work from home for the rest of the day. As she made her way toward the elevator, her phone buzzed; the call was from an unknown number. Ignoring it, she let it ring, choosing the silence she could only provide herself.

Once settled in her car, Mocha released a turbulent tide of tears, each drop symbolizing the release of pent-up frustration and anxiety. She gripped the steering wheel tightly and braced herself for the uncertainty ahead: a daunting journey into the unknown. She wondered why she had chosen to reopen such deep wounds, especially since she had closed this chapter in her life long ago.

Deep down in her heart, Mocha knew she needed this and deserved to know. Wiping the tears from her eyes, Mocha glanced at herself in the rearview mirror. She took a cleansing breath and spoke these words to herself as she had done many times before: "Setbacks are not failures. They are opportunities for us to reevaluate our assignments." As these words permeated her spirit, she could hear Montana's words: "Such cases can be lengthy and take a toll on individuals." Mocha had to see this through, regardless of the outcome.

Mocha was not in a good headspace and knew working from home would be unproductive. Therefore, she opted to take a short ride to Chesapeake Beach to reevaluate her next move. The thought of the salty breeze and the sound of waves grazing the rock against the shore gave her hope. As she navigated the winding roads, she envisioned sitting on the warm sand, taking a moment to clear her mind and reassess her next steps in her personal and professional life. The peaceful scenery would provide her with the clarity she desperately needed.

Mocha sat on the pier, watching the sun begin to descend behind the clouds, casting vibrant hues of crimson and gold across the sky. The clouds, tinged with shades of lavender and deep orange, danced delicately in the warm evening breeze, creating an exquisite tapestry reflected on the tranquil waters below. It provided the most beautiful sunset she had ever seen. Gathering her belongings from the weathered bench, Mocha headed to her car and prepared to return to the city.

Upon returning home, Mocha engaged in her evening routine, which included taking a shower, preparing a cup of ginger and lemon tea, and settling into her California King-sized bed. After silencing her phone earlier, she took a moment to check for missed calls and voicemails. Among them, she found a voice message from Kingston McIntosh, whose voice she recognized immediately. Although she felt hesitant about returning his call, Mocha placed great emphasis on holding others accountable for their commitments —a principle she had instilled in herself since childhood.

The next morning, Mocha rose early to review her work emails and make a call to Kingston. Just as she was about to dial his number, her phone buzzed. The caller introduced herself as a representative of Solar Technology. She wanted to confirm Mocha's availability for the following week. They settled on next Tuesday at noon. After the call ended, Mocha began to dial Kingston's number; however, an inner voice redirected her, and she dialed Jaxzon's number instead.

As she waited for him to answer, she could hear his rich, baritone voice enveloping her like a warm blanket, soothing the deep ache in her heart. She closed her eyes, envisioning him pulling her close and whispering comforting words that promised everything would be alright. The phone rang three times before going to voicemail. She left a message in the hope that he would return her call.

Mocha dialed Kingston's number, and he answered on the first ring. "Good morning, Ms. McBride," he greeted warmly. "I hope you're doing well. First, I want to sincerely apologize for not following up with you as I promised during our last meeting. I understand how important timely communication is in our line of work." There was a brief pause before he continued, "The executive team has reviewed your proposal, and after careful consideration, they have decided to invite you for a face-to-face meeting at our headquarters in Toronto. This meeting will provide an opportunity for us to discuss your ideas in greater detail and further explore potential opportunities for collaboration.

Mocha was surprised by Kingston's unexpected response. She mentioned that she would follow up to confirm both her and Journee's availability for a meeting. After consulting with Journee, they decided to schedule the meeting for three weeks from now. Mocha shared Harlan's direct phone number and email address with Kingston to facilitate communication regarding her flight itinerary and accommodation arrangements.

After her conversation with Kingston, Mocha had expected to feel a surge of excitement at the news and the promising opportunity that lay ahead. Yet, instead of exhilaration, a profound emptiness settled within her, as if the very prospect that should have sparked joy left her feeling hollow and unfulfilled. She wanted to believe it was due to the events that had transpired over the past few days, but something felt off in the pit of her stomach. She shrugged it off as a result of her nerves.

The phone rang just minutes after she had hung up with Kingston, the echo of their conversation still lingering in her mind. It was Jaxzon calling. As she saw his name flash across the screen, a rush of emotions washed over her—anticipation mixed with uncertainty. Mocha felt speechless, her heart racing as she struggled to gather her thoughts. She quickly answered the call before it went to voicemail.

"Hello," she said, trying to sound calm and not nervous.

"I hope I didn't catch you at a bad time."

"No, I just wrapped up a business call. My apologies for not hearing the phone ring earlier; I was out for a sprint around the neighborhood." It has been a while since we last spoke. How are you? Jaxzon asked. I have been very busy with these new projects. What about you? I just returned from a trip to Virginia, where I had the pleasure of meeting several relatives from my father's side of the family. We gathered at an old family estate surrounded by lush greenery, sharing stories of our ancestors over soulful meals. It was wonderful to reconnect with cousins I hadn't seen in years and hear about their lives and experiences. The warmth of their hospitality and the sense of belonging made my visit truly memorable.

As Mocha listened to Jaxzon speak about his visit with his family, she felt a deep sadness and a hint of jealousy in her heart. She wished she could experience that. "It sounds like family means a lot to you," Mocha said. Jaxzon could hear the sadness in Mocha's response and chose not to ask any questions about her family. So, do you have any dinner plans for tonight, Jaxzon asked. No, Mocha replied. Well, now you do. They planned to meet at a restaurant in Anacostia, a neighborhood in Southeast Washington, D.C., at seven.

Chapter 9

UNRAVEL

Journee Arielle Sullivan stood in her apartment, the city's mid-morning light slanting through tall windows and casting soft shadows on her parquet floor. Her mind wandered as she recalled how she had learned early on to smile with her eyes, even when her heart ached. It was a talent developed out of necessity, not choice—honed through countless foster home transitions, courtroom hearings, and whispered conversations she wasn't meant to overhear.

By the age of six, she had already memorized the look adults wore when they realized her mother wasn't coming back. It was a softening in their eyes, a slight tilt of the head: pity, concern, dismissal.

Now in her thirties, Journee sat in the plush leather seat of a first-class cabin on her way from Los Angeles to Atlanta, watching the clouds float like secrets too weightless to hold. Her reflection in the window stared back—sharp cheek-bones, caramel-toned skin, wide-set eyes that once brimmed with questions and now burned with ambition. She was the very definition of poised success:

a senior partner at one of Atlanta's top law firms, known for her surgical courtroom precision and relentless pursuit of justice.

But beneath the tailored suits and courtroom victories lived a girl with no last name to trace, no bedtime stories passed down, no family recipes etched in memory.

The layover in Dallas was unexpected—a reroute due to weather in Atlanta. She had barely stepped off the plane before she spotted a familiar figure in the terminal, her sandy brown curls and mocha skin unmistakable even from behind.

"Mocha McBride," Journee called, voice lilting with nostalgia.

Mocha turned, her eyes widening before breaking into a grin. "Journee Sullivan, girl, I cannot believe it. You look the same!"

The two women embraced tightly, laughter blooming between them. Mocha had been one of the few constants in Journee's chaotic teenage years. They met in a group home outside Decatur, Georgia, bonding over shared silence and stolen moments of freedom. After high school, they drifted apart—life tugging them in different directions. But the memory of Mocha's warmth, her fierce loyalty, remained anchored in Journee's heart.

Over lattes in a quiet corner of the airport lounge, Journee and Mocha tried to catch up on what had happened over the years. They both agreed to stay in touch, and they had. When Mocha mentioned that she was looking for her family, it felt like a punch to her gut. She had also begun searching for her family and discovered secrets that were meant to stay hidden.

***

It started with her birth certificate. The state redacted most of it but left breadcrumbs—small pieces. Just enough to follow the trail. The name was hidden in court records from her intake file. She had to pull a few strings to access it. Journee's heart raced. She retrieved her phone and opened a scanned image of a birth index. There, in faded typewriter font:

Journee Arielle Ballard. Born: July 7, 1991.

Mother: Liza M. Ballard.

She could not understand why her last name was listed as Ballard on this birth index, yet she goes by Sullivan.

Journee felt the world tilt beneath her, the ground shifting like buried fault lines. She had hoped the search would bring closure, perhaps even joy. Instead, it unraveled a tapestry she hadn't realized she was woven into. Journee felt the weight of history pressing on her shoulders. What had started as a quest for identity was now a minefield of secrets. Her heart ached with longing for family, for clarity, for connection—but she knew the truth would demand a price. And she wasn't sure who would pay for it.

Journee ran a hand over the cluttered surface of her desk, scanning the scattered documents—photocopies of social service records, handwritten timelines, names circled in red. She had once approached this search like a legal case: objective, precise, and detached. But now, every file was personal. Every fact was a potential emotional inferno.

She pulled out the manila folder she had labeled "LMB – CONFIDENTIAL" and flipped it open. Inside was the cornerstone of her search: a notarized intake form from 1991, stamped by the Georgia Department of Family and Children Services. Scribbled in a corner were the words, *"Mother refused to name father. No known relatives."*

Journee scanned her phone and pulled up an email she had received just days before from a private investigator in Macon:

From:trivers@peachstateinvestigations.com
Subject: Update on Birth Mother Search – Liza M Ballard

"Journee, I found a sealed file connected to a domestic violence incident from 1991. The file is restricted, but I have a contact in Augusta's courthouse. The mother—Liza—was admitted to University Medical Center just two days before your intake into the foster system. I believe the two events are connected."

Journee sat back, heartbeat thunderous. If Liza had been injured or hospitalized, it could explain the disappearance. Maybe she hadn't abandoned her. Perhaps she'd been unable to return. But why would that file be sealed? Her mind raced.

Journee stood and crossed the room to a small safe nestled in her bookshelf. She unlocked it and pulled out the only physical relic she had from her biological mother: a thin silver bracelet engraved with three initials—*LMB*. She had found it tucked into the lining of the duffel bag she was dropped off with as a child. No one had ever claimed it. She clenched it tightly. "Augusta," she murmured aloud. "That's where the answers are." Journee knew this wasn't a time for hesitation. She had survived the system. She had survived, not knowing. She would survive the truth.

CHAPTER 10

TRIGGER

Maxwell's meeting with Tristan did not unfold as he had anticipated. Instead of a casual one-on-one conversation, he found himself facing a panel interview that included several high-ranking executives from the company, all of whom held significant decision-making power. To his surprise, his former boss, with whom he had worked closely for over four years, was also present among the panelists.

The atmosphere was charged with a mix of formality and intensity as questions flew at him from various directions, each executive scrutinizing his responses and assessing his fit for the new role. Maxwell felt a heightened sense of pressure as he realized that this meeting could determine the trajectory of his career.

He left the meeting feeling unnerved, as he did not handle surprises well. Feeling bombarded, he went outside to get some fresh air and collect his thoughts. Once he returned, Tristan, along with his executive assistant, requested to speak with him privately.

Maxwell felt a wave of anxiety wash over him after the last meeting, the echoes of raised voices still ringing in his ears. The fluorescent lights of the office flickered above as he walked toward the boardroom, and his heart raced, each thud a reminder of his mounting dread.

It felt as though the walls themselves were inching closer, suffocating him in an invisible grip. This situation triggered his deep-seated fear of the unknown, an ever-present shadow that loomed over him whenever uncertainty struck.

As he approached the heavy wooden door of the boardroom, Maxwell began to replay the meeting in his mind, each detail sharper and more vivid, as if it had just taken place seconds ago.

. The tension, the feeling of—it was a chilling reminder of the fire experience that echoed the symptoms of post-traumatic stress disorder he had been grappling with for some time.

Before he could bravely step into the boardroom, he felt an overwhelming urge to pause. He ducked into the nearby bathroom, the cool, tiled floor a brief respite from the chaos swirling in his head.

Closing the door with a soft click behind him, he crouched down with his back pressed against it, seeking solace in the small, enclosed space. Taking a deep breath, he focused on happy memories: the sound of his daughter's laughter on a summer day, the warmth of his partner's hand in his, the peaceful mornings spent with a cup of coffee and a good book.

In this moment of quiet reflection, he reminded himself that this meeting was merely a test of his resilience and that he had the strength to weather this storm. As he gathered his thoughts, he felt a glimmer of hope shine through the anxiety, preparing him to face whatever awaited him beyond that door. Wiping the sweat from his brow and adjusting his tie, he turned the knob of the door to face his fate.

Maxwell entered the boardroom, where Tristan sat at the head of the table with his assistant to his right. "Have a seat," he said as Maxwell approached.

Pulling out his chair, he tried to read their faces before sitting down. “Would you like something to drink?” his assistant asked. Maxwell replied, “No, but thank you.” “I know you’re wondering why I asked you to come back,” Tristan said—and equally wondering why so many people were in on this meeting. “Well, Maxwell, your name has been the topic of many discussions since you were asked to take on this project a year ago. You have exceeded and outperformed seasoned executives in the company. That being said, we would like to offer you the position of regional director, responsible for the offices I currently oversee. We do not expect an answer today, but we look forward to hearing from you before the end of the fiscal year, which, as you are aware, is in July.

Tristan leaned forward and extended his hand toward Maxwell, a confident smile on his face. “Do you have any questions for me before we wrap up?” he inquired, his tone friendly yet professional. As they shook hands, Maxwell felt a firm grip that conveyed assurance. After Tristan and his assistant turned and walked out of the room, the door clicked shut behind them.

Maxwell remained seated at the polished oak table, staring at the spot where Tristan had just stood. Time seemed to stretch on endlessly; the silence of the room enveloped him like a heavy blanket. He was at a loss for words, still processing the significance of the conversation they’d just had.

Finally, he exhaled deeply, releasing the tension that had built up in his chest. As he sat there, a wave of excitement began to wash over him, his mind racing with possibilities. Thoughts of new opportunities and challenges filled his head, and he couldn’t help but let a small smile break across his face.

Chapter 11

HIDDEN

Montana reviewed the documents he received from Mocha. Many of these cases involving foster care or the search for a loved one are lengthy and complicated. As he delved deeper into Mocha's case, it became increasingly clear that the narrative she had been given was filled with inaccuracies.

The stark contrast between the reality documented in the files and the story Mocha had been led to believe highlighted the profound misunderstandings that often accompany such deeply personal matters. This revelation only fueled Montana's determination to uncover the truth, as he recognized its significant implications for Mocha's future.

In light of the case's complexity, he reached out to his close friend, Savion, for assistance. Given Savion's extensive expertise in this field, he knew they would have a better chance of solving the mystery.

Savion pored over the documents and immediately recognized several similarities he had encountered in previous cases. One of them was that the birthplace was unknown, with both the mother's and father's first and last names left blank, raising questions about the individual's origins and family background. This lack of information suggests a possible adoption, abandonment, or other circumstances that could have obscured their identity.

Additionally, the last foster home placement that Mocha had mentioned did not exist in any of their databases. For all intended purposes, nor did Mocha. Montana pondered in disbelief how Mocha's very existence could have remained concealed for such an extended period, perplexed by the layers of secrecy that shrouded this remarkable being.

When Montana asked Mocha if she knew why her birth certificate did not include her parents' first and last names, Mocha hesitated, gathering her thoughts. She could only recall fragmented snippets of conversations she had overheard while staying at the Engel's home; however, those memories were hazy at best. Yet, she could not answer why it did not include their names. What she said afterward melted his heart.

Mocha remembered sitting on the weathered porch of the old house where she had been abandoned, the lingering scent of summer flowers mingling with the distant sound of traffic. A concerned neighbor, noticing that she had been there for quite a while and it was getting late, finally decided to call the police. Mocha realized that the sound of sirens marked a turning point in her life and still affects her to this day; answers about her family remain elusive.

Savion collected all the documents from Montana and noted that he needed more time to review them thoroughly. He was confident that he would have some concrete information for him in a few days. Montana and Savion agreed to meet in two weeks to discuss their findings.

Montana understood that Mocha's childhood trauma profoundly affected her ability to recall many events from her past. This reality was mirrored in the name that lingered in his mind: Bettie Jo Engels. Intrigued, he ran a search on her name in the police database, which revealed that she was living in Silver Springs, Maryland.

Curiosity piqued, he delved deeper into her background and discovered a troubling history: Bettie had been released from probation a few years earlier for a case involving serious allegations of child abuse, neglect, and endangerment. The details painted a clear picture; the case garnered media attention due to its shocking nature, revealing a pattern of abuse that left irreversible pain on her victims.

As he pieced together this information, Montana felt a chill run down his spine; he sensed that uncovering Bettie's past might be crucial to unraveling the mysteries surrounding Mocha's own traumatic experiences. He wrote down her last known address, booked an open flight to Washington, D.C., and rented a car. While he was there, he planned to visit Bettie Jo and Mocha.

Montana was on his way to the office when he received a call from his lead investigator, Sarah Martinez. Her urgency was palpable as she informed him that she had obtained crucial new intel about Mocha's case—intel that could potentially shift the entire course of the investigation. "We need to act fast, Montana," she urged, her voice steady but laced with tension. As he pulled over to the side of the road, his heart raced, knowing that every second counted in unraveling the complexities of the case that had haunted him for weeks.

CHAPTER 12

SHADOWS

Mocha felt like she was on cloud nine after her delightful dinner with Jaxzon. They had decided to meet at a cozy restaurant on Monday evening, known for its eclectic menu featuring both seafood and hearty soul food. The atmosphere was warm and inviting, with soft lighting and the gentle sound of jazz playing in the background.

Each dish they sampled was a delight, bursting with flavor, and their engaging conversation flowed effortlessly between them. As they shared laughs and stories, the chemistry between them deepened, making the evening memorable in many ways. Neither of them noticed the patron seated across the room, watching them with an unreadable expression.

After dinner, they decided to stroll through the vibrant neighborhood streets of Anacostia, appreciating its rich African American history and unique architectural style. They agreed to return on the weekend to visit Frederick Douglass's home and explore all the notable attractions Anacostia offers.

Mocha arrived home just before midnight, the quiet streets barely echoing her footsteps. With a soft sigh of relief, she dialed Jaxzon's number to inform him that she had arrived safely. After a brief conversation, she stepped into a warm shower, letting the water wash away the day's fatigue before sinking into her cozy bed, as the world outside faded into silence.

The next morning, she prepared for work as the sun rose gently. When she stepped outside, she paused to bring in her trash can, enjoying the cool morning air against her skin. As she walked to the mailbox, disappointment struck her again—there was no mail once more. Frowning, she reminded herself to stop by the post office to inquire about it.

Upon arriving at work, Harlan set up the PowerPoint presentation and ordered lunch for her meeting with Solar Technology. The meeting went smoothly, with their Vice President, James Jackson—a seasoned executive known for his strategic insights—and Kerina King, the lead software designer, recognized for her innovative problem-solving approach. The atmosphere buzzed with excitement as they engaged in a lively discussion about the potential for future collaboration.

Mocha left work early to reach the post office before it closed. As she walked to her car in the parking lot next to the building, her phone rang; it was Journee. Their conversation was brief, as she was traveling out of town for business and wanted to check in on how the meeting with Solar Technology had gone. Mocha also updated her about her dinner date with Jaxzon. She arrived at the post office with only ten minutes to spare. After speaking with the clerk, Mocha learned that the postal carrier assigned to her route was currently on vacation and would return on Monday. However, she assured Mocha that she would keep an eye on her mail until he got back.

Mocha had not slept for the past three nights; her mind raced every time her alarm went off at the crack of dawn, relentless in its shrill insistence. This would be her third service call in just two days, each one echoing with frustration as the technicians combed through her home, checking outlets and testing circuits, only to leave empty-handed. She held her breath during each visit, hoping for a resolution, but each time they departed, they found nothing unusual.

The lack of sleep was taking a toll on her both emotionally and physically. She was grateful that the mishaps with the alarm system had occurred after her meeting with Solar Technology. Harlan knocked on her door to inform her that a package had been delivered for her in the conference room. Mocha was surprised because she hadn't expected any deliveries.

When she arrived at the conference room, a beautiful bouquet of red and white roses sat on the table. Mocha's heart melted at the sight; it was truly a delightful surprise. Her first thought was that it must have come from Jaxzon, but she quickly dismissed that idea, as he did not know where she worked. Mocha searched for a card, but there wasn't one. "They are beautiful," Harlan said. "Don't let me find out you have a secret admirer." Mocha smiled and took the flowers into her office. Puzzled by the unexpected gift, Mocha was curious about who had sent it.

The end of the week finally arrived, and Mocha felt a wave of relief wash over her. After a long week filled with back-to-back meetings and deadlines, she was particularly excited about the prospect of unwinding with Jaxzon. They had planned a cozy evening together, complete with her favorite takeout from that little Thai place down the street and a movie marathon of their go-to classics. The thought of sharing laughter and perhaps a few inside jokes made her heart race with anticipation, reminding her of the warmth and comfort his presence always brought.

Jaxzon called just before the driver left the garage, confirming her address with a note of excitement in his voice. The ride from Glen Burnie was smooth, taking about twenty-five minutes as they navigated their way through the tree-lined suburban streets.

Mocha had just picked up takeout along with a bottle of rich red wine. After placing the food on the table, she retrieved elegant glassware from the cabinet, the clinking sound echoing softly in the cozy dining room. Suddenly, she was interrupted by the sharp bark of a dog. It was a familiar sound—the neighbor's golden retriever often barked at passing cars or whenever a deer wandered into their yard, nibbling on fallen acorns. But for some reason, his barking grew louder as if he were in distress.

Mocha walked to the lanai and opened the sliding door. The motion sensor immediately activated. She grabbed the shovel resting against the wall and headed toward the rustic ten-foot fence that bordered the back end of her property. Mocha strolled along the tree line of the yard and spotted what appeared to be footprints, which she presumed belonged to the employees from the alarm company, along with what she thought were deer tracks or those of a small animal. Just as she was about to open the gate, her phone rang, and it was Jaxzon.

"Hello," she said. "I'll be arriving at your place in less than two minutes," Jaxzon replied. After ending her call with him, Mocha heard her neighbor calling for their dog, and the barking stopped. Sprinting into the house, she quickly glanced at herself in the mirror before heading to the front door.

The floodlight illuminated as the car pulled into the driveway. Mocha waited for Jaxzon to ring the doorbell because she didn't want him to think she was overly eager and anxious, standing at the door, even though that was exactly what she was doing. All Mocha could do was laugh at herself. Why was she trying to impress him? After all, the version of her that truly mattered was to be authentic.

Opening the door, Jaxzon stood there with a warm smile, a dozen red roses, and a bottle of wine. "Come in," she said, her voice inviting as she stepped aside to let him enter. Mocha led Jaxzon into the kitchen and offered him a seat at the island while she searched for a vase for the roses. "So, what's on the menu?" Jaxzon asked. "I ordered Kang Keaw Wan Kai, Pad Thai, Spring Rolls, and Tom Yum," and none of the dishes were cooked in peanut oil or contained any. He smiled and offered to set the table and pour the wine. Mocha suggested they eat their meal in the living room while they watched movies.

Mocha had several movie options spread across her coffee table, and Jaxzon, with his easy smile and warm presence, knelt beside her to help with the choice. After some playful debate, laughter, and teasing, they settled on a double feature of "Boyz n the Hood" followed by "Black Panther." The lights were low, and the scent of Thai cuisine mingled with Mocha's lavender candle. As the first movie played, the distance between them on the couch slowly disappeared.

By the time the credits rolled on *Black Panther*, it was one in the morning. Mocha turned to find Jaxzon watching her instead of the screen, his gaze soft yet intense. The air between them shifted, charged with something beyond friendship. She smiled a bit nervously and said, “It’s late. You should probably stay. The guest room is already prepared.”

Jaxzon didn’t answer immediately. Instead, he brushed a stray curl from her face and asked, his voice low, “Are you sure that’s where you want me to stay?”

Her heart pounded as she held his gaze. “I don’t know,” she whispered. “Should it be?”

He leaned in slowly, giving her time to pull away—but she didn’t. Their lips met in a gentle, exploratory kiss that deepened with a tenderness neither of them expected. The walls Mocha had built around her heart trembled, not from fear, but from the possibility of something real.

Later, as the first light of dawn peeked through the curtains, they sat wrapped in a blanket on the couch, her head resting on his chest, fingers intertwined, the TV forgotten. What started as a movie night had become the beginning of something more.

CHAPTER 13

THE SEALED ROOM

Journee arrived at the University Medical Center in Augusta, Georgia, just before noon. She was not dressed in her usual courtroom attire but chose a more casual look, featuring dark jeans and a leather jacket, accompanied by a determined expression. The sound of her heels echoed in the tiled corridor as she walked to the Medical Records Department for a meeting with Trevor Rivers, a private investigator from Macon.

She stood at the front desk, arms crossed tightly against her chest, her brow lightly furrowed in a mixture of impatience and determination. The receptionist behind the counter, with a weary yet practiced expression, approached her with a faint smile that barely masked her fatigue. "Hello, how can I help you today?" The receptionist's voice carried a tone that suggested she had encountered many like her—those seeking elusive files that seemed to stay shrouded in mystery, hidden away from prying eyes.

"Hello, my name is Journee Sullivan. I have a meeting with Trevor Rivers at noon." Yes, he called and mentioned that he would be meeting you today.

He has run into some traffic, but he will be here shortly. Journee turned to take a seat. Twenty minutes later, the waiting room door swung open, and a middle-aged gentleman stepped inside. He carried himself with an air of confidence, his neatly combed silver hair contrasting with the deep lines etched on his forehead, hinting at a lifetime of experience. With a warm smile, he intro-duced himself as Trevor Rivers.

The receptionist, who had been organizing medical charts at the front desk, looked up and recognized him immediately. She gestured toward Journee, her voice soft yet clear, indicating that she was the person he had come to see. Journee glanced up, her curiosity piqued, as she felt a mix of anticipation and nervousness as their eyes met.

Good afternoon, Ms. Sullivan, it is a pleasure to finally meet you. Likewise, Journee said. They briefly spoke about the case as an older woman with sharp eyes and a cautious tone approached, advising that she would escort them to a private room in the basement archives.

"Most of this was sealed by court order," the archivist said. "But your names appear on the patient file—Journee, as 'infant present during a domestic incident,' and Ashley Davenport, as next of kin to Liza M. Ballard. That allows us to show you a summary."

She slid a beige folder across the table and left the room.

Journee opened it with reverence.

The file was brief—just a three-page summary of events from July 1991. A domestic violence report. A visit from Child Protective Services. A premature labor scare. And then a note:

Patient: Liza M Ballard

Admitted: July 5, 1991

Discharge Date: July 8, 1991

Observation: Signs of sustained trauma. Refused to disclose the attacker.

Requested placement for the child in protective care under an alias.

Journee's hands trembled. "She gave me up to protect me," she whispered. Journee leaned over, eyes wide. "Wait. What's this?"

At the very bottom of the page was a red-stamped line, faded but legible:

Note: Refer to file B-1197 to Dr. V. Sutton – clearance approved for counseling.

"V. Sutton?" Journee said slowly.

Journee stood, backing away from the table. Her voice was a whisper of disbelief. "Could Dr. Sutton be the key to this mystery? Or, Ashley, the next of kin."

With focused determination, Journee leaned closer to the archivist, who had returned, her voice low and insistent. "Could you please provide me with any additional information? Perhaps the name of the attorney involved or details about the social worker who handled the case?" Her heart raced at the thought of uncovering buried truths, yet the archivist's weary sigh hinted at frustration.

"I'm sorry," the archivist replied, glancing at the cluttered desk and then back at Journee, disappointment etched on her face. "I don't have anything else in the records. What's here is all we've got." The words hung in the air, heavy with unspoken stories waiting to be told. Journee sensed some deception in what the archivist had said. She leveraged her legal credentials and immediately summoned her supervisor.

Trevor could see the frustration etched on Journee's face, her brow furrowed, and lips pressed together in a thin line. Sensing the tension in the air, he approached her gently and asked if she would mind stepping outside for a moment while he navigated the situation inside. Journee hesitated, glancing at the bustling waiting area filled with anxious faces, but ultimately nodded and complied, her heart racing with doubt.

Approximately thirty minutes later, Trevor emerged from the consultation room, his expression grave and burdened. With a heavy sigh that seemed to weigh down the very air around him, he made his way to Journee, who was seated in the uncomfortable plastic chair, her foot nervously tapping a rapid rhythm against the cold, tiled floor.

He extended his hand toward her, gently placing a small, crumpled sheet of paper into her palm. The paper felt cold and lifeless, a stark contrast to the warmth of her anxious grip, and it served as a chilling reminder of the distressing news it contained. As Journee unfolded the paper, her breath caught in her throat, anticipation and dread flooding her senses.

CHAPTER 14

ASHES AND ECHOES

It had been a few weeks since Maxwell received the promotion offer to become the Midwest regional director. Despite the enticing salary increase and the added prestige of the role, he still wrestled with uncertainty about whether to accept it. As he weighed his options, memories flooded back of late nights spent with his team, the camaraderie they had developed, and the thrill of collaborating on innovative projects. Yet, the prospect of increased responsibilities, long hours, and potential conflicts with his current peers loomed large in his mind.

Maxwell found himself reflecting on how this decision would impact his work-life balance and mental well-being, and whether he was truly prepared to embrace a more demanding leadership role. Each passing day deepened his internal conflict, prompting him to consider which path would best align with his career goals and personal values. He decided that driving to the gym would be a good way to relieve stress and clear his mind. He grabbed his gym bag, protein drink, and electrolyte packs that he would need after an intense workout.

The grueling two-hour workout was exactly the mental reset he needed, though the enticing job offer still loomed over him like a shadow, leaving him in a state of indecision. Each repetition had pushed him to his limits, filling him with a rush of endorphins that made him feel invigorated yet contemplative.

As he finally pushed open the door to his car—a comforting sanctuary amid the chaos of his thoughts—his phone vibrated insistently in his pocket, breaking the momentary silence. Glancing at the screen, he saw an unknown number flash before him. Unsure whether it was a friend reaching out, a misdial call, or a co-worker seeking an answer, he opted to let it go to voicemail, cherishing the peace of the moment as he gathered his thoughts for the choices ahead.

Maxwell made a right turn into the neighborhood and immediately thought of Mocha. He hadn't seen her in a few weeks and assumed she was either working late or out of town. As he passed her house, he noticed an unfamiliar car pulling into the driveway. This was unusual; during his year of living in the neighborhood, he had never seen anyone else visit Mocha's home. His curiosity piqued, he wondered who might be stopping by and if Mocha was okay. However, Maxwell reminded himself that he was overstepping. She was a responsible adult, and she was neither his partner nor his responsibility. But, in the back of his mind, he wished she were.

He had just finished showering and was getting ready to make something to eat when his phone rang. He answered without checking the caller ID and instantly recognized the familiar voice on the line.

Maxwell had grown up numb. Hardened. Hollowed out.

And now, after years of silence, a voice from the past cracked through his phone like thunder on dry earth.

"Max?" The voice was tentative. Jerrod.

Maxwell froze. His grip on the phone tightened.

"Hi Max, it's been a long time since we last spoke. Has it been four or five years? That's far too long for siblings not to talk."

"I… I found out where you were. I just wanted to talk. See you."

Maxwell's chest tightened. He could hear the echo of their shared childhood in that voice—the whispered stories under threadbare blankets, the plans to run away, the last hug before the system tore them apart.

***

Maxwell Vaughn hadn't slept through the night in over six years. Not since the fire. Not since the screams. Not since the world he knew—what little of it he had dared to love—was swallowed whole in a blaze so cruel it scorched the marrow of his soul. His partner, Alana, and their daughter, Payton, only five years old, had been taken from him in a fire the investigators still hadn't explained. *Faulty wiring,* they said. *Accidental ignition.* But Maxwell knew differently. He *felt* it in his bones—something about that night had been off. The silence before the blaze. The way the hallway light flickered as if warning him. The shadowy figure someone claimed to have seen fleeing the alley behind their brownstone. A truth buried, twisted beneath bureaucracy and grief.

Now, every night was a battlefield. The scent of burning wood lingered in his dreams, often waking him in a cold sweat, heart pounding against his ribs like a trapped animal. He'd reach for them in the dark—Alana's warm breath against his shoulder, Payton's tiny feet thumping down the hallway for morning cuddles—but there was only air. Silence. And the sickening ache of absence.

Maxwell lived in a quiet bubble. The human connection had become a luxury he didn't trust. Even his brother, Jerrod, had stopped trying. The last time they spoke, it ended in shouting, blame hurled like bricks. Jerrod never understood Maxwell's silence, his retreat from the world after the fire. But Jerrod hadn't been there. He hadn't lost *everything.*

Maxwell's childhood was a facade, a slow-burning tragedy. His father was an alcoholic who was skilled at delivering backhanded insults and physical punishment. His mother, fragile and often absent, vanished when Ma Maxwell was ten, leaving behind two children and a whirlwind of unanswered questions. Jerrod coped by being loud, visible, and successful, while Maxwell chose to remain invisible. He learned early on how to stay quiet and navigate life from the shadows. However, simply surviving did not lead to healing.

It was why, at thirty-eight, he had no real friendships. No family dinners. Just routines—late-night walks, black coffee in chipped mugs, and isolation. An illusion of possibilities of what life could be. He was slowly healing and could see a tiny ray of sunshine on the horizon. Her name was Mocha.

Mocha McBride was like jazz in a silent room—confident but not arrogant, warm without expectation. Her laughter carried, sometimes reaching him despite the thick scar tissue around his heart. For the first time in a long while, Maxwell began to think that healing might not come from forgetting, but rather from allowing someone to witness the ashes.

***

Maxwell listened as Jerrod spoke of reconnecting and meeting. They talked about their childhood. About the pain. About Alana and Payton. About trying to survive in a world that often didn't seem built for people like them.

"I never stopped wondering about you," Jerrod said.

" Maxwell admitted quietly. "I had to."

But reconciliation, like grief, is not linear. And while Maxwell and Jerrod began the slow process of mending their bond, another presence lingered on the edges: their sibling. The unnamed one. The one who was supposed to be born in secret and left behind without even a cradle to their name. Maxwell felt Dr. Patel's words resonate within him, planting a seed of hope that he could navigate this transition and emerge even stronger on the other side. Maxwell and Jerrod planned to meet for dinner in a week.

The next day, Maxwell awoke early, the soft rays of dawn filtering through his curtains and casting a warm glow over his room. He stretched lazily, a content smile spreading across his face as he mentally reviewed the errands he needed to tackle. With a cup of steaming coffee in hand, he gazed out the window as he watched his neighbor walk his dog.

As he prepared to step out, he couldn't shake off the thoughts of his overdue conversation with Jerrod that lingered in his mind. It wasn't just any chat; it felt more like an unresolved melody playing softly in the background, its rhythm unexpectedly discordant. Maxwell had anticipated a straightforward discussion, but the complexity of their relationship as brothers had transformed it into something far more intricate. As he closed the door behind him, he wondered how their dialogue would unfold and whether it would bring the clarity he yearned for.

As he drove past Mocha's house, he couldn't help but notice that the sleek, black sedan he had seen parked in the driveway the night before had vanished. With a mental checklist of errands swirling in his mind, he resolved to swing by Mocha's place later in the day to check in on her. After all, their friendship was important, and he wanted to make sure she was doing all right.

CHAPTER 15

THE KNOCK

Montana met with Sarah shortly after their phone call and invited Savion to join them for the meeting. Sarah mentioned that she had been working on a case similar to Mocha's. She took the initiative to speak with Savion beforehand, and he reviewed the relevant documents before their scheduled meeting.

Sarah handed over the file she had meticulously compiled, her expression a mix of anticipation and concern. Montana stared down at the worn, leather-bound folder resting in her hands, its cracked surface reflecting years of frequent handling—a testament to the stories it contained. Inside lay two lives intricately woven together by a complex tapestry of secrets, hidden bloodlines, and a mother's desperate attempts to shield her daughter from the harsh realities of their tumultuous world.

As Montana carefully opened the folder, the faint scent of old paper and traces of ink filled the air, evoking a sense of nostalgia and intrigue. He revealed yellowed pages covered with meticulously typed documents, interspersed with hastily scrawled notes that hinted at a past filled with turmoil, resilience, and heartbreak. Each piece of paper seemed to whisper stories of hidden truths and buried legacies, drawing him deeper into the labyrinth of their shared history.

The common thread binding this intricate narrative was the name Dr. V. Sutton, a figure who seemed to loom large in both lives, shrouded in mystery yet pivotal to their story. With every detail Montana absorbed, a picture began to form—a narrative full of unanswered questions, waiting to be unraveled.

***

The Arizona heat was dry but heavy, pressing against Montana's skin like a judgment. His shoes crunched softly over the gravel as he stepped out of the rental car. The air tasted like dust and desert sage, the sky above an unflinching blue. He stared at the small adobe cabin in front of him. It wasn't much, but it didn't have to be. What mattered wasn't the place—it was the woman inside.

Potentially Mocha's mother.

Montana's hands were slick with sweat, though his face remained unreadable. He'd practiced what he might say a hundred different ways on the flight here. He walked the final steps toward the door and paused. The cabin was quiet. No movement behind the curtains. No footsteps on the floorboards.

He raised his hand and knocked. The sound echoed through the canyon like a heartbeat. Silence followed. Then— Footsteps. Soft. Slow. Cautious. The door creaked open. And there she was. Samira Townsend.

Montana stared at the woman who had given Mocha life.

"Hello, how can I help you?" she asked, her voice steady but tinged with concern as a flicker of worry crossed her face.

"Good morning, ma'am. My name is Montana McGee. I'm looking for Samira Townsend."

Samira hesitated before responding. "What is this about?" she asked.

"It's about a baby you gave up over thirty years ago named Mocha. "Samira blinked back tears. She took a step back, her hand resting on the doorframe for balance, allowing Montana to enter the cabin.

The cabin was dim and cool, filled with the scent of dried flowers and old paper. On a table near the window sat a worn leather journal. On the mantle, a single photograph: a baby in a hospital bassinet, with a pink name tag that simply read *Baby Girl Thomas*. Montana stared at the picture. "She looks just like her father," she whispered, voice like a tremor in the wind. "But her eyes... those are mine."

Montana's throat tightened, and Samira's eyes filled with tears. "I left her with everything I had. I had nothing else to offer her, and I didn't want to leave her in the environment I was in." "Please, sit down," she said. Samira offered Montana a glass of freshly brewed sweet tea with lemon and a slice of lemon pound cake.

Mr. McGee, I do not know where to begin. Samira said.

Montana sat across from her, hands folded in her lap. There was no dramatics in her posture. No performance. Just a woman, stripped bare by the truth she was finally ready to tell.

"I was twenty-two when I met her father," she began. "He was older, charming, and in a way, dangerous that I didn't yet know how to name. I thought he saw me," Samira continued. "I was broken, rebellious, half-homeless, running from a house that had never known peace. Then this man came along with his deep voice and empty promises. I didn't know he was married. I didn't realize I was just a distraction."

"When I found out I was pregnant," Samira said, "he told me to handle it. Said he had a life to protect. A name." Her jaw tightened. "I refused. I told him I'd keep my baby." A bitter laugh escaped. "That's when it turned violent." "He hit me," Samira whispered. "The night I told him. He said if I ever spoke his name or showed my face in his world again, I'd disappear—and so would the baby."

Montana could feel his heartbeat in his throat.

"I ran," Samira said. "I found a shelter two states away. I gave birth in silence, under an alias. No birth certificate with my name. No trace."

She swallowed hard. "I was so scared. Not just for myself. For *Mocha*. I knew he had power. Money. People. I knew if he found out I kept her; he might take her—or worse. So, I called one person I trusted—Veronica."

"She was working in Georgia by then. She arranged a closed adoption, something that would keep the records sealed. But at the last second... I couldn't go through with it. I changed my mind. I wanted my baby. I *needed* her."

"Then why didn't you keep her?"

Samira choked on her breath. "Because he found me again."

A silence fell over them, heavier than before.

"He found me three weeks after I gave birth. He left a message on the door of the shelter. My name and the hospital. A threat, carved into a piece of wood: *One word from you, and she's gone.*"

"I left that night," Samira whispered. "I put her in foster care temporarily—just until I could find a safer place. But the system moved faster than I could. And I... I broke. I couldn't think. Couldn't act. I kept watching from a distance, terrified that if I got close again, he'd finish what he started."

Montana's lips parted. "Who is he?"

Samira didn't blink. "Mocha's father's name is *Judge Aldric McBride*."

Montana's blood ran cold. He felt like he'd been punched in the chest. He looked down, then toward the door, where Savion and Sarah stood outside. He turned slowly back to Samira. "Say that again." "I said... her father is Aldric McBride."

Montana stood, hands trembling, heart pounding in his ears. His voice shook. "Mocha's father is *Aldric McBride*."

Montana was overwhelmed with heartbreak for Samira and Mocha. For the first time in years, he felt a profound sadness for them. An emotional weight pressed down on him, leaving him at a loss for words as he witnessed their pain unfold. He struggled to express the deep sorrow that enveloped him, feeling completely unable to find the right words.

Montana knows Judge McBride in a professional capacity, having interacted with him through his work with the court. For years, rumors have suggested that he favors younger and more impressionable individuals. The idea of him exploiting someone in that way made him feel physically ill.

CHAPTER 16

BUILDING BLOCKS

The following weeks unfolded like a slow-burning melody—as Mocha and Jaxzon found themselves spending more time together, naturally falling into each other's rhythm. Their connection deepened beyond the confines of her living room couch and late-night movies. They began to explore the world just outside her door, hand in hand, curiosity guiding them.

Jaxzon and Mocha returned to the National Museum of African American History and Culture in Washington, D.C., pausing in reverent silence as they stood before exhibits that echoed ancestral pain, resilience, and pride. Jaxzon watched Mocha absorb each artifact, her expression a mix of fire and grace. When she wiped a quiet tear from her cheek, he gently wrapped an arm around her shoulders and held her close without saying a word. His presence was steady and grounding.

They spent time back in Maryland, as they strolled the cobblestone streets of Old Town Alexandria, stopping for coffee and warm cinnamon pastries from a tucked-away bakery. They laughed over shared memories and marveled at how their paths had aligned. Later that weekend, they attended a jazz night at a cozy lounge in Baltimore, where a live band played smooth grooves under dim lights. Mocha wore a flowing emerald dress, and Jaxzon couldn't take his eyes off her. When he pulled her onto the dance I'll floor, they swayed like they'd been dancing together for years—his hand at the small of her back, her head resting on his shoulder.

The following weekend, they visited Monticello in Virginia, and the conversation turned reflective. On the drive back, as golden light spilled over the highway, Jaxzon reached for her hand and glanced over. "Can I ask you something?" he said, his voice laced with sincerity.

Mocha nodded, sensing something different in his tone.

"I want to know you, beyond what we've seen and shared. Tell me about your family... where you come from. And what do you want for your future?"

Mocha took a deep breath; her eyes fixed on the trees zipping past the window. "That's a layered question," she said softly. "Family has always been complicated for me. I've often felt like a chapter missing its beginning. I never knew my parents and grew up in foster care starting at the age of seven. I have no baby pictures and no bedtime stories. When I was sixteen, I met my dear friend Journee—she's more like a sister to me. I aged out of the system at eighteen, and my first year of college felt like I was intruding on everyone else's family narrative. But for the most part, I learned to build my own village." That's why I hired —Montana McGee. He's one of the best private investigators in the southeastern region. He's digging through old records, trying to find anything that leads me to where I came from. It's terrifying... but necessary."

Jaxzon squeezed her hand. "And what do you envision for yourself, ten years from now?"

"I want to create something lasting," she said after a pause. "A thriving business that helps young women find their voices through creativity. Maybe write more, travel, and love deeply. I want peace that doesn't need to be earned."

She turned to him. "And you? Where do you see yourself?"

He smiled quietly. "I'm focused on building a life that matters. I work in solar technology and conservation, primarily for nonprofit housing developments. My goal is to restore spaces that, in turn, help restore people. I hold a degree in civil engineering from the University of Cologne, with a minor in air quality and solid waste management. Beyond my work, I aspire to create a home filled with laughter and love—a place where I have a partner who challenges me and loves me unconditionally." What about your parents? Mocha asked.

My parents divorced when I was in my second year of college. I am the only child, so growing up was sometimes lonely. And equally hard due to my mixed heritage of Afro-German background. My father was stationed in Germany in the Army when he met and married my mother. They were extremely young and were not equipped to navigate a world that only saw color, not love. Mocha felt a tug at her heartstrings as she listened to him speak of his parents.

Their eyes met once more, and the silence between them was charged with mutual respect, shared dreams, and something unspoken yet deeply felt. "You might have just described my heart," Mocha whispered. He took her hand and pressed a kiss to her wrist. "Then maybe... we're already building something real." In that car, somewhere between the roads of Virginia and the plans for tomorrow, they realized they were slowly drafting the blueprint for something extraordinary—together.

Mocha now at home after being dropped off by Jaxzon. She began preparing for her upcoming trip to Canada. During this time, she has been reflecting on her recent communication challenges with Journee. The two have not spoken in over two weeks due to conflicts in their work schedules, which have led to missed opportunities for connection. When they did manage to have conversations, they often felt rushed, and Mocha found her to be preoccupied. Despite this, Mocha did not express concern, recognizing that Journee, a high-profile lawyer, has a demanding and stressful job.

As she packed the last items into her luggage, the doorbell rang. She saw Maxwell standing there with some mail in his hand. When she opened the door, she greeted him with a warm smile and thanked him as she reached for the mail.

"Maxwell, I'm truly sorry for my mail continuously being delivered to your house," she said, her voice filled with a mix of embarrassment and concern. "I reported the issue to the post office weeks ago. They assured me that the regular carrier was on vacation but should have returned by now." She took a deep breath, glancing around nervously. "It's not a huge problem, but I wanted to check on you anyway, as I haven't seen you in a while and wanted to make sure you were okay."

Puzzled by his comment, Mocha stepped back, her heart racing. Was he watching her? An uneasy feeling settled in her stomach like a heavy stone. It couldn't just be a coincidence that she had been experiencing strange issues with the alarm system lately. She couldn't shake the feeling that there was more to this than meets the eye. Mocha insisted that she needed to leave, as she had something cooking on the stove and didn't want it to burn.

After closing the door behind her, she quickly ran to her surveillance system and reviewed the footage from the past month. What she saw was nothing out of the ordinary, so she thought. Unease settled over her, and she decided to get some dinner at the bistro. Just as she parked her car, her phone rang, and it was Montana. They had not spoken in weeks, so she was eager to hear what he had to say.

"Hi Montana," she said, her voice trembling with a mix of anxiety and hope. "I hope this call brings me some news, preferably good." The air was thick with tension as she awaited his response. After what felt like an eternity, he finally spoke, his tone serious yet gentle. "There have been some developments in the search for your parents."

Mocha struggled to grasp the deeper meaning behind Montana's words. Frustrated, she turned off the engine and opened the windows, letting in a cool breeze that swept through the car, refreshing the stuffy interior that had grown heavy with unspoken tension. At the moment Mocha was preparing to ask Montana about his findings, the call was abruptly disconnected. Despite multiple attempts to dial Montana's number, all calls went directly to voicemail.

Mocha found herself anxiously attempting to contact Montana well into the depths of the night, her mind racing with concern. As dawn broke, she reached out to her trusted friend Loren, sharing the unsettling events that had unfolded. A knot of fear twisted in her stomach at the thought that something could have happened to him.

Understanding the urgency of the situation, Loren promptly informed her boss, who immediately set out to check on Montana's well-being. Later that evening, with a mix of relief and lingering worry in the air, Loren called Mocha to deliver the news. She told her that there had been a break-in at Montana's office. He had pursued the intruder and suffered minor injuries during the chase, but he was now safe. The tension of the night gave way to a sense of relief, but the shadows of the incident still lingered.

CHAPTER 17

WHIRLWIND

It had been two weeks since Journee met with Trevor Rivers. She had not been able to sleep or eat and was on an emotional rollercoaster. Glancing at the crumbled piece of paper, he gave it to her while at the University Medical Center. The solitary word scrawled across it— "*ALIAS*"—echoed in her thoughts, gnawing at her sanity. Her mother's name, she now suspected, was not *Liza M. Ballard*. Frustration and despair wrapped around her heart like a vice, leaving her feeling just as lost as she had been six months ago when she embarked on this daunting quest for the truth.

Trevor and Journee met at a bookstore about a mile from her workplace to discuss the additional information he had found regarding her case.

"The name *Liza M. Ballard* didn't exist before 1991," he said. "No birth record. No high school transcripts. No tax returns, social security number—nothing."

Trevor slid a worn document toward her. "Your mother's real name is *Lilliana M. Banks.* Born in New Orleans in 1975. Went missing in 1991—right around the time you were born."

Journee blinked. "Banks?"

Trevor gave a nod. "And here's where things get complicated." He pulled out another page—this time, a scan of a black-and-white photograph. Two women, arms slung around each other, smiling in front of a worn-down brick shelter. The edges were yellowed with time. On the back, someone had scribbled *CeCe & Liza- Haven House, 1991.*

Journee leaned forward, her breath catching in her throat.

"That's my mother?" she whispered.

Trevor nodded. "And the woman next to her is *CeCe Thomas.*"

Journee's heart jumped. "Thomas"

"Yes," he said. "Her bunkmate."

She stared at the photo. "Lilliana had come to the shelter after fleeing an abusive relationship." He tapped the picture. "This photo was taken at a shelter in Georgia. Both women were pregnant. Both were hiding from their abuser."

Journee froze.

The room tilted.

Journee sat back in her chair, her lungs tight with disbelief.

"Lilliana gave birth to you and went on the run. CeCe gave birth shortly after.

Journee felt bile rise in her throat. Lilliana wasn't just hiding from him. She was hiding from *what he did to her."*

Trevor leaned closer, his tone solemn. "These men destroyed more than one life. Your mother changed her name, cut off contact with everyone—including CeCe —and lived in fear for decades. You were her line in the sand. Her last chance to break free."

Journee's hands shook as she lifted the photo again. Her mother looked *young* in it. Carefree. Unscarred.

"Do you know what happened to Ce Ce's child?" she asked.

Trevor hesitated.

"That child," he said carefully, "was placed in foster care. The records are sealed. She leaned forward, eyes wide, voice cracking. Journee sat in stunned silence, the truth sitting heavy on her chest. So many pieces. So many lies. And all of it leads back to men who were cowards. So, there was no mention of the fathers in the records. No, Trevor said, but I am still looking, and I will find them.

"Can you find Lilliana?"

He gave a slow, measured nod.

"I'll try. But if she's alive... she's been hiding for a long time. It'll take time."

Journee stood, the photo still clutched in her hand.

"I have time," she said.

She looked toward the door, toward the blazing Georgia sun beyond the bookstore's shadow.

"I have plenty of time, but the man who is my father does not."

CHAPTER 18

INVESTIGATOR TACTICS

Montana had returned from Arizona on Sunday and was at his office to follow up on some additional information he had received from Samira. Just as he began to dial Mocha, the lights in his office flickered. A gust of cold air swept through—odd, considering the windows were closed. He tensed. Something was off.

Montana's instincts had saved him more than once in this business, and tonight, they were screaming. He reached for the Glock tucked under his desk drawer just as the front door rattled open with a *crack*.

"Who's there?" He called out.

Silence.

He moved like a panther at six feet three inches and two hundred thirty pounds, quiet and ready. Stepping lightly into the front office, he saw it—the shadow of a figure slipping out through the back fire exit, fast and calculated. His eyes darted to the cork board.

The folder marked *"McBride"* was gone.

Montana ran to the alley and caught a glimpse of a black hoodie disappearing into a waiting car. He didn't get a plate, but he saw something else.

A burn mark on their left hand.

It wasn't random. Whoever that was, they hadn't come to rob him. They came to disrupt the truth. They came to bury what was about to rise.

Back inside, Montana paced, thinking quickly. He had digital backups, thank God. But the message was clear.

Someone doesn't want Mocha to find her mother.

Montana picked up his phone and dialed Mocha directly—no time for pleasantries. "Mocha," he said the second she answered, breath sharp. "Listen to me. We need to meet. In person. There's more, and it's not safe to talk on the phone."

Mocha, startled, sat up in bed beside Jaxzon. "What's going on? What happened?"

"I think someone's been watching us. Watching *you.* I don't know who, but they've already made a move."

Jaxzon, hearing Montana's tone, leaned in. "Put him on speaker."

Montana continued, voice calm but urgent. "Mocha... your birth mother is alive. I know where she is. But someone doesn't want this truth to come out. Be careful who you trust. And whatever you do, don't go anywhere alone."

***

Across town, a few days later, in a shuttered mechanics garage on the edge of Capitol Heights, *a figure* stood over the stolen folder, flipping through Montana's notes. Their jaw clenched as they read *Samira Townsend's* name.

So that's where she came from...

The pieces were moving faster now. But they weren't worried. Chaos was their art form. If they wanted the past, they'd give it to them. But not how they expected.

They pulled out a Polaroid from their pocket. A faded photo of Maxwell, Jerrod, and a girl who looked suspiciously like Mocha, only younger, smaller, sadder.

They carefully set the photo ablaze, placing it within an old, battered coffee can, and watched as the flames flickered and danced, the embers soaring like secretive whispers into the night. All that lingered in their minds was a smile—a hollow curve that never quite reached the depths of their eyes. It was the same façade they'd mastered to navigate the twisted labyrinth of foster homes, indifferent social workers, and therapists who remained oblivious to their silent cries. It was the smile of a survivor, a hardened mask forged from pain, transforming their scars into fierce weapons of resilience.

Pulling the photos from the vanilla photos on the desk, they smirked as they ran their finger along the edges. —Mocha laughing with Jaxzon on the steps of the Smithsonian, holding hands outside a jazz lounge, conversing with Maxwell while standing on her driveway.

She had them all.

And it festered like acid in their chest.

To them, Mocha was the thread that pulled it all apart. She was there when the system stepped in. She lived while others *survived*. She dared to smile, to *thrive*, while I *was* erased in the shadows.

“They seek the truth?” they murmured, their voice barely rising above the crackling flames. Shadows danced around them, flickering in the dim light. “Then let them have it.”

They had no intention of letting Mocha find peace. They believed peace was for people who didn’t leave others behind. They didn’t get to rediscover their roots while they were left digging through the ashes of their life.

So, they made the call.

“Yo,” a gravelly voice answered on the third ring. “It’s time,” they said. “The girl, the PI, and that damn lawyer. I want eyes on them all. No slip-ups. No mercy.” You want the same heat as last time?” the voice asked.

Their eyes narrowed, flashing with cruel memory. “No. That was personal. This time? It’s surgical. Scare them. Shake the ground under their feet. Let her know her past ain’t hers to claim.” I want them to suffer like I did. I do have something specially planned for each one of them.

They hung up and stared at the wall, where the burn mark from a candle licked halfway to the ceiling. They lit another one now, carefully watching the flame dance.

“Mocha,” they whispered. “You started this when you tore us apart. And I’ll finish it. One person at a time.”

CHAPTER 19

I REMEMBER

Vivid memories began to surface as Maxwell prepared to meet Jerrod in just a few days. He was only ten years old when his mother knelt to kiss him goodbye, her lips brushing against his forehead as she whispered softly, "Be good, my prince." With those words, she walked out the door, leaving behind a world tinged with uncertainty that would never return. She never came back. Left to navigate a grim existence with his younger brother, Jerrod, they were placed into the chaotic care of a father whose presence was shrouded in the stench of cheap whiskey and simmering rage.

The brothers bore bruises that blossomed like dark, painful flowers beneath their tattered shirts, a testament to the volatile atmosphere of their home. Night after night, the air filled with the haunting echo of screams that reverberated through the thin, cracked drywall of their childhood home, each cried a plea for help that went unheard. It wasn't until Child Protective Services intervened that their fragile lives began to shift; the brothers were abruptly torn apart, ripped away from each other as if they were mere fabric being pulled apart, leaving them feeling frayed and incomplete.

Jerrod was taken to a foster home that felt foreign and cold, while Maxwell was placed with a different family, each boy thrust into the broken machinery of a foster care system that offered little solace. Their unnamed younger sibling, an unconfirmed secret born of their mother's desperation, vanished into the system like a shadow swallowed by dusk, slipping away without a trace and leaving an aching, untold memory. Maxwell vividly remembers the promise he made to Jerrod. "I promise. Wherever they send us, I'll find you. I'll always find you."

But promises made in chaos are fragile things. The years blurred after that—files misplaced, letters undelivered, birthdays missed. And eventually, silence.

Maxwell buried the guilt deep, focusing instead on survival. On work. On Alana and Payton. On pretending that life could still be kind. But grief, like a stubborn wound, never truly healed.

The brothers met two days later at a quaint diner nestled just outside the Capitol. Jerrod had visibly aged; the lines on his face bore the marks of a weary resilience, a testament to battles fought and survived in a hellish struggle. Yet, within the depths of his eyes flickered a warmth, a glimmer of the spirited bond they once shared, hinting at a flicker of hope amidst the shadows of their past. They talked for hours. They both realized that they hadn't searched as hard as they should've. They had allowed the system to erase their bond—until now.

A few nights after their reunion, Jerrod called again, his voice heavy with something unspoken.

"You remember when Mom left us?" he asked. "Of course I do."

Maxwell exhaled. "Hard to forget."

Jerrod hesitated. "Did you ever wonder if we were the only ones?"

"What do you mean?"

"I found something, Max. After she left... after they took us... I tracked down one of the old case workers. She said our mother had a baby. After us. A year later. But not by our dad. Different man. Someone she met after she left us."

Maxwell's mind reeled. "You're saying we have a sibling out there?"

"We *had* a sibling all this time. And we never knew. They were born into the chaos. She left them behind, Max. And no one ever talked about it. Not even you."

Maxwell was silent. He hadn't known. Not truly. Yet, there were whispers—faded fragments of phone calls between case workers when he was too young to understand. A reference to "the infant" that made no sense at the time. He'd buried it. Like everything else.

Jerrod's voice dropped lower. "I think that sibling has been trying to find us. I think they already have."

A knot formed in Maxwell's chest. "What do you mean?"

"I saw someone watching us at the diner. Not just glancing—*watching*.

CHAPTER 20

TRUST

Mocha sat on the edge of her bed, replaying the conversation she had with Montana, her phone vibrating silently in her palm like a ticking bomb. "They took the file, Mocha. Someone broke into my office. I think we're both being watched."

She replayed the line over and over. *They took the file.They're watching us.*

A chill crept up her spine. She pulled her robe tighter around her body and paced to the window, peeking through the blinds. The street outside was quiet, too quiet—like the world was holding its breath.

Jaxzon stirred on the couch in the living room, where he had fallen asleep watching old documentaries. His presence, once comforting, now made her stomach tighten. She had known him for barely five weeks. Their connection had been passionate, surprising, and deep—but how deep was it really, and how much had she filled in with hope?

What if he isn't who he says he is?

Montana's words echoed louder now. "Don't go anywhere alone. Be careful who you trust." Mocha backed away from the window, heart hammering against her ribs. Every face in her world suddenly blurred at the edges. Maxwell was someone whom she was already suspicious of. She was told the mail mix-up was a clerical error. The alarm system malfunctioned, just a glitch. But what if it wasn't? And now this trip to Canada, to meet with Kingston McIntosh. But instead of feeling excited, Mocha felt her throat tighten every time she thought about crossing that border.

She walked into the bathroom, turned on the faucet, and splashed cold water on her face. Staring at her reflection, she whispered, "Who can I trust?" And then there was *Montana,* the only person who seemed to want to uncover the truth. But even he was vulnerable now. His office in Tennessee had been violated and ransacked by a ghost who moved with purpose.

Mocha tiptoed back into her bedroom and grabbed her journal. She flipped through its pages—sketches, phrases, dreams, and a long list of unanswered questions.

She jotted down three names:

- *Jaxzon* – Stranger or Sanctuary?
- *Maxwell* – Questionable?

Her eyes drifted to the third name she didn't want to write:

- *Samira Townsend* – Mother?

That word still felt foreign. Sharp. Fragile.

Her phone buzzed again. Another message from Montana.

“I’ve confirmed it—Samira’s expecting you. She’s nervous. Said she’s never stopped praying for the little girl she lost. Please, Mocha... don’t delay too long.”

Mocha bit her lip, tears stinging the edges of her vision. She looked over at her suitcase, already packed for Canada. The passport was on top, tucked under a scarf. The weight of her choices pressed down on her chest.

To go meant moving forward. But forward felt like walking blindfolded into the fog, unsure of who walked beside her... and who waited in the dark.

She closed her eyes, whispered a quiet prayer, and clutched her pendant—something she’d kept since she was a child, though she never knew where it came from. A simple bronze butterfly.

“God,” she breathed, “if You’re still writing my story... I need you to take the pen right now.”

Outside, the streetlight flickered.

And somewhere in the night, a camera lens blinked once... then disappeared into the shadows.

The next morning, Mocha awoke to the sound of the alarm buzzing, and light streamed through the blinds, casting long golden lines across the hardwood floors. The smell of fresh coffee drifted from the kitchen, but it did little to calm the unrest stirring in Mocha’s chest.

Jaxzon stood at the stove, shirtless, humming quietly as he stirred something in a pot.. He looked at peace. Too much peace. Mocha leaned against the doorway, arms folded. Her eyes studied him—not with admiration this time, but calculation. The kind you develop after life has taught you that love sometimes hides its claws behind a kiss.

“Morning,” he said with a smile. “I made ginger tea, scrambled eggs, bacon, and toast. “She nodded slowly. “Thanks.” He moved toward her with a mug, but she didn’t take it right away. “Can we talk first?”

Jaxzon’s smile faded into something more serious. He set the mug on the counter. “Of course.” Mocha pulled out a stool and sat, never taking her eyes off him. “Do you... really have feelings for me, Jaxzon? Or was this just convenient?” The question cut through the room like a blade. He leaned against the opposite counter, arms crossed.

“I care about you, Mocha. Deeply. I wouldn’t be here if I didn’t.”

“You’ve been here, sure,” she said, voice tight. “But this is getting real. Dangerous. People are watching me. Someone broke into Montana’s office. My file was stolen. And it all ties back to me. My past.” Jaxzon exhaled slowly. “I heard you on the phone last night.”

“Then you know why I’m asking,” she said. “Do you see a future with me, or are we just in some romantic fog that’s going to clear the second things get hard?”

“I didn’t grow up in fairy tales, Mocha,” he said. “I know life gets hard. That’s the part I’m actually built for. But I also know you’re going through something that’s forcing you to question everyone around you. And I don’t blame you for including me in that.”

She nodded, but her expression didn’t soften. “So, what’s your plan?” she asked. “Where do you stand in all this?” He walked over and gently placed his hand over hers. “I stand *with you.* But if you need space to figure that out for yourself, I won’t take it personally. Just don’t shut me out completely—not if there’s still a chance for us.”

She stared at his hand, then up into his eyes, searching for cracks. She didn’t find any. But she also didn’t find the answer she needed most: certainty. “I need to know if I can trust what we’re building,” she whispered.

"I'll show you," he said. "Not just say it."

Later that morning

Mocha sat in her car, staring at her phone before finally dialing. "Journee? Hey, girl." Journee's warm voice filtered through. "Hey! I was thinking about you. Are you still set for Canada next week?"

"That's why I'm calling. There's a lot going on. My PI's office was broken into. Someone's been watching me... maybe even tailing me."

Journee's tone shifted instantly. "What?! Mocha, are you okay?"

"I'm... processing. Trying not to panic. But I need someone I trust to be with me in Canada. I'm meeting Kingston McIntosh, and I think you being there would give me peace of mind."

"Of course, I told you I would go. Say no more. But, uh... You might want to know something about Kingston."

Mocha blinked. "What do you mean?"

"I've been doing some digging since you first mentioned him. And I came across a few red flags. I was speaking with a colleague a few days ago, and his company came up regarding a merger, and this did not come up in our meeting with him." And there was mismanagement of capital, causing a layoff of over one hundred employees.

Mocha's heart sank. "Why didn't you tell me earlier?"

"Because I wasn't sure. But now with everything going on, I'd rather you be too cautious than caught off guard." Mocha gripped the steering wheel. "So, he might not just be an opportunist. He might be connected to this somehow."

Journee paused. "Mocha, do you think he could be tied to whoever's watching you?" "I don't know," she whispered. "But I'm not ruling anything out anymore." As she hung up, Mocha looked at her reflection in the rearview mirror.

This wasn't just about finding her mother anymore. It was about *surviving* the truth.

And the more she uncovered, the more she realized—

The most dangerous lies were the ones told in love, in family... and in silence.

CHAPTER 21

SMOKE SCREEN

Maxwell sat on the edge of his bed. No matter how many windows he opened, how many nights he stayed up trying to forget, he could still hear Payton's laughter, still see Alana's silhouette in the kitchen doorway just seconds before everything turned to ash. He stirred his coffee absently. Cold.

A knock came at the door—sharp, deliberate, then silence. He opened it to find no one standing there. Just a plain manila envelope on the welcome mat. No return address. His gut tightened. Maxwell picked it up, scanned the street, then shut the door and locked it. He sat at the table and slid the letter out. The paper was thick. Expensive. And typed in all caps.

YOU'VE BEEN LOOKING IN THE WRONG DIRECTION.

THE FIRE WASN'T RANDOM. IT WAS RETRIBUTION.

TELL ME, WHY WOULD SOMEONE KNOW ABOUT THE GAS LINE UNDER THE STOVE? OR THAT THE SMOKE DETECTOR BATTERIES WERE REMOVED THE NIGHT BEFORE? OR THAT PAYTON'S FAVORITE STUFFED ELEPHANT WAS FOUND SOAKED IN LIGHTER FLUID—IN HER CLOSET? ONLY YOU AND THE FIRE MARSHAL WERE GIVEN THAT REPORT. SO, ASK YOURSELF, MAX: WHO ELSE WOULD KNOW… UNLESS THEY WANTED YOU TO?

THERE BACK. AND THEY NEVER FORGOT THAT YOU LEFT THEM BEHIND.

Maxwell read it three times before his hands stopped shaking.

The police report had been sealed. Restricted to official personnel and him. Those details were never made public. Not even Jerrod knew the full scope. And now someone was not only referring to him—they were *weaponizing* him.

He turned the letter over. No fingerprints. No markings. But that last line...

They never forgot that you left them behind.

OH MY GOD, PLEASE DO NOT LET IT BE TRUE!

Maxwell reached for his phone and scrolled to Detective Brian Hale; the only person left at the precinct who still owed him a favor. "I need to look at the fire files again," Maxwell said the moment he answered. "They've already been reviewed, Max. It was an accelerant—open flame, no forced entry. I thought we closed this." "Well, reopen it," Maxwell said grimly. "I got a letter. With details no one should know. Unless they were there."

There was silence on the other end. "I'll pull the file," Hale said. "But Max... if you're right... you're not dealing with grief anymore." Maxwell's jaw tightened. "I know." He stared at the letter again. The words burned hotter than any flame ever could. Because he realized *THAT* the secret was a reality, and his sibling they were playing a game built on silence, fire, and vengeance.

Maxwell called Jerrod and filled him in on the letter and asked him to set up a meeting with the caseworker. Maxwell rubbed his temples, heart pounding.

Silence stretched between them, heavy with the realization that the past wasn't behind them—it was circling.

Maxwell closed his eyes and remembered that last moment outside their home—the promise, Jerrod's tiny hand clutched in his, and the hollow sound of their mother walking away.

Now there was another hand in the dark. One they had never held. One that had grown alone in the cracks of their broken story.

And it was reaching back, not for love or reunion—

But for revenge. And was this revenge in plain sight.

CHAPTER 22

DISTANCE AND DIRECTION

The morning after their talk, Jaxzon stood at the edge of Mocha's porch with his overnight bag in his hand. The sun hadn't yet climbed above the rooftops, but the air was already tense with everything left unsaid.

Mocha met him at the door, arms crossed over her chest, eyes guarded yet soft.

"You don't have to go," she said.

"I know," he replied. "But I think you need space. And I need clarity."

She nodded slowly, grateful that he didn't try to force his way into her uncertainty. He leaned forward and kissed her forehead—nothing demanding, just a quiet affirmation that he saw her. All of her.

“I meant what I said, Mocha,” he murmured. “I’ll show you who I am. No pressure. No pretending. Just time and truth.”

And with that, he left.

Two Days Later – Richmond, Virginia

Jaxzon stepped into the sunlit office of his modest but growing consulting firm—Nova Element Solutions, a boutique innovation firm focused on sustainable infrastructure and renewable energy development. His visit to the States was not just for pleasure but for business. He set his laptop down and dialed his secretary, Malika, a whip-smart Howard alum with a steel-trap memory and zero tolerance for mediocrity.

“Morning, Jax,” she said. “You’re off the grid for two weeks, and suddenly your inbox is screaming. What’s the game plan?”

“I need you to schedule a strategy session,” he said. “I want to revisit our solar tech proposal—especially that partnership with the Department of Environmental Quality in Maryland. And loop in the conservation contacts from Northern Virginia.”

Malika didn’t miss a beat. “The renewable infrastructure bill is gaining traction in the state senate. If you get your prototype pitch ready by next quarter, we could attract big investment, especially with your European credentials.”

Jaxzon nodded, pacing. “And schedule a call with Dr. Hendrik Weber in Munich. He’s working on solar glass models—ultra-lightweight panels for low-income housing. If we can adapt that model here, I want us to be first in line for licensing.”

“You thinking community-centered solar grids again?”

“Exactly,” he said. “Long-term impact. Low-cost. Cultural equity. We build where we were forgotten.”

"Damn," Malika said with a grin in her voice. "You back on your visionary sh*t."

Jaxzon smirked. "That's the only way I know how to move."

After the call, he sat down at his desk and opened a folder labeled *Legacy Projects*. Inside were sketches, market analysis, community proposals, and a mission statement he'd rewritten a dozen times:

"Empowering tomorrow by rebuilding today—one roof, one panel, one life at a time."

He ran a hand over his beard, the weight of purpose settling on his shoulders.

He missed Mocha. That was the truth.

But giving her space didn't mean abandoning her. It meant becoming the man who could stand beside her when the time was right.

The man who wasn't just chasing love but building something worthy of being loved.

Later That Night

Jaxzon sat on his balcony, watching the city flickering in the distance. He tapped out a message but didn't send it.

Mocha, thinking of you. I hope Canada brings you more clarity than confusion. I'm still here. Quiet, but close.

Instead, he saved it to drafts. Some messages weren't for pressure or persuasion. Some messages were just reminders that love doesn't always shout. Sometimes, it waits.

A week later, Jaxzon needed to travel back to Germany for a crucial meeting with Dr. Weber to review the prototypes he had developed for the new project in the States, and this also gave him the chance to check in on his parents.

After his parents' divorce, his mother moved to Munich to be closer to her sister. The familiar smell of cloves, citrus, and fresh bread wrapped around Jaxzon like a wool blanket the moment he stepped into his mother's apartment. The floors creaked with memory; the walls hung with sepia-toned photos and African textile prints his father had once collected during his Army tours.

His mother—Claudia Jeffries—was already bustling in the kitchen, humming low and off-key, just the way she always had.

"Mein Sohn," she said with a warm smile, drying her hands on a towel as he entered. "You're too thin. America isn't feeding you properly."

Jaxzon laughed and opened his arms. "I missed you, Mama."

They hugged tightly, then sat at the small wooden table where countless conversations—light, hard, and unforgettable-had been shared.

She poured tea into two mismatched mugs. "So. You've come all this way with more than jet lag, haven't you?"

He hesitated, stirring honey into his cup. "There's a woman."

Claudia's eyes twinkled. "There's always a woman."

"No. This one's different."

He spoke slowly, choosing each word with care. He told her about Mocha—how they met, how she moved with passion and purpose, how she challenged his logic and softened his edges. And then, how she had recently begun to pull away. Not out of rejection, but survival.

"She's searching for her birth family," he said quietly. "She just found out her mother was alive. There's been danger, break-ins, and lies from the past rising like smoke. She doesn't know who to trust."

"And you think she doesn't trust you," Claudia said, always quicker than he expected. "I don't blame her," he admitted. "I came into her life fast. She's unraveling something ancient. I didn't grow up without parents—I grew up with one who stayed, and one who left by choice."

Claudia grew quiet at that.

"She asks questions about you," Jaxzon added. "About why you divorced. Why did you never fight harder to stay together as a family?"

Claudia stared at her tea.

"I loved your father," she said softly. "But the world didn't love us. Not here. Not there. We thought our love would be enough for you. And I thought staying in Germany would protect what little strength I had left."

She looked at him now, her eyes misting. "I was wrong. I missed so much of your life as you were chauffeured between two homes. I should have fought harder."

Jaxzon reached across the table and covered her hand. "I don't hold it against you. I just... want to do it differently. With Mocha."

"Then do it," she said. "Even if she pushes away. Love her without needing her to choose you first. Be the one person she doesn't have to question."

He nodded, letting the weight of her words settle into his heart.

After a moment, Claudia said, "Tell me more about her."

"She's layered," he said. "Resilient. Creative. She sees the world like it owes her nothing but still gives it everything. But there's sadness there too—a wound that never fully healed."

He paused. "I think she's scared that everyone she loves will eventually leave. That love always ends in fire."

Claudia sighed. "Then be her water. Not to fix her... but to stay near the flame and not run." Claudia felt her son's pain as she knew firsthand how secrets had caused the flame in her marriage go out.

CHAPTER 23

THREADS IN THE DARK

Trevor Rivers never liked missing pieces. He'd been a private investigator long enough to know that the most dangerous secrets were always the ones hiding in plain sight. And lately, this case—this ever-expanding network of women, lost children, sealed files, and institutional betrayal—had begun to feel less like an investigation and more like a reckoning.

He sat at his desk long after midnight, a wall of documents pinned behind him. Names. Dates. Photographs. Threads. Some red. Some black. All of this leads back to a central figure. It was on the *other* names buried in the medical record from Augusta—names that hadn't fully registered at first. Names like:

Dr. Veronica. Sutton – Attending Psychiatrist
Ashley Davenport – Emergency Contact, Secondary Kinship Placement Application

Trevor narrowed his eyes. Veronica M. Sutton. That name had resurfaced elsewhere—in connection with child placement logs tied to an old group home in Fulton County. A name linked to two boys, Trevor's hands froze.

The surname Banks was already present—Journee Arielle Banks.

He pulled out an archived intake form from 1999. Two boys and two girls were placed into emergency foster care after an alleged domestic disturbance and parental neglect. No father listed. Mother disappeared.

Next of Kin: *Ashley Davenport,* relation – *maternal cousin.*

Trevor stared at the connection, his heart rate rising. So that was it. Ashley Davenport had taken emergency custody of Journee, but the placement hadn't lasted. After two months, Journee was placed in the system. He leaned back, exhaling. That meant Ashley Davenport and Veronica Sutton were connected to Journee's *and* these two boys' bloodlines—if not by parentage, then by protection. Veronica had quietly supported the placement after Lilliana's disappearance.

Trevor reached for another folder—his own. He flipped through files and stopped on one labeled:

Vaugh, Maxwell D. – Former Resident, Haven Path Transitional Housing

That name wasn't just a professional interest anymore. Maxwell was a boy lost to the system, buried in silence after their family had been split apart years ago. Maxwell and Jerrod were brothers. It was Veronica M. Sutton. Her name was also connected to the boys through placement files, psychiatric notes, silent signatures, and sealed court documents. She hadn't just helped Journee, Maxwell, and Jerrod survive; she had also helped *conceal* them. Trevor picked up his phone; it was time to make the next call to Veronica to confirm his suspicion.

Trevor waited in the sun-drenched corridor of the psychiatric unit at Emory Midtown, the echo of quiet footsteps and distant intercoms bouncing off the polished floor. The woman he had been trying to locate for weeks—Dr. Veronica M. Sutton was finally within reach. He wasn't here for a confrontation. He was here for the truth. And she knew it.

A nurse directed him toward the consultation room. When he entered, she was already there. Impeccably dressed in charcoal gray slacks and a pressed blouse, her silver-streaked hair swept neatly back. Her eyes—piercing and composed—met his with an almost defiant calm.

"Mr. Rivers," she said. "I wondered when you'd find me."

CHAPTER 24

NEW TERRITORY

Mocha had spoken with Montana, and he suggested rescheduling her trip to Canada as he feared for her safety. She assured him that she was not traveling alone, that Journee would be accompanying her. She provided Montana with her lodging accommodation, itinerary, as well as Kingston's contact information.

Mocha and Journee arrived in Toronto, Canada, late afternoon. The city welcomed them with a sky like brushed steel and a brisk wind that curled around their coats. Mocha stepped out of the black sedan, her boots hitting the pavement like hesitant punctuation marks. Journee was right behind her, sunglasses low on her nose, scanning the area like a bodyguard more than a best friend.

The city felt... off.

Too many cars were idling with their drivers still inside. A man across the street was pretending to read a newspaper, though the pages never turned. A silver SUV that had been behind them for the last four blocks.

Mocha's senses were sharp now—no longer lulled by the romance of reunion or the sparkle of discovery. They entered the marble lobby of the upscale boutique hotel where Kingston McIntosh had booked their stay at the Bristol Hotel, Private Conference Suite. It was too elegant, too carefully curated. Every employee had a practiced smile. Every flower arrangement was perfectly symmetrical. They were being watched. She could feel it.

Mocha tossed her bag onto the bed and paced, running her hand through her curls. "You saw the car too, didn't you?" she asked. Journee nodded, her face serious. "The gray Acura? Yeah. Same one that trailed us out of the airport. Either they're security—or they're something else."

Mocha collapsed onto the bed, exhausted but vibrating with adrenaline. "Montana said my file was stolen. That we were being watched. I didn't expect it to follow me *across borders.*"

Journee sat across from her and leaned forward. "There's more I haven't told you." Mocha looked up sharply. "I've been doing my own research," Journee continued. "I have also been in search of my mother. Trevor Rivers is the private investigator I hired. A few weeks ago, he was able to give me the name of my birth mother. Trevor is still in search of her as she went on the run after leaving an abusive relationship to keep me safe." Mocha instantly sat up in bed. She was speechless but instantly saw a sadness in Journee's eyes. And as her friend and sister she needed her support. Mocha approached Journee and gave her a hug. No words were exchanged just complete silence.

A low, deliberate knock on the door echoed through the suite causing Mocha and Journee to release their embrace of one another. They exchanged a glance—cautious, alert. Journee stood first and peeked through the peephole. "It's Kingston," she confirmed. "Alone."

Mocha took a deep breath and nodded. "Let's do this." Kingston stepped into the suite like he owned every room he entered. Tall, deep-toned, his suit was flawlessly tailored, his voice slick with charm and curated intellect.

"Ladies it is good to see you again. You are more radiant since the last time we met." His flattery felt too rehearsed. Too polished. Mocha forced a smile. I hope the accommodations are satisfactory. Kingston said. Yes, they are Mocha replied. Great. I will meet you in the conference room tomorrow morning at ten.

As Kingston turned to leave, Mocha caught a flicker of movement in the hallway. Two men in street clothes one nodded subtly at her, just once. Mocha quickly closed the door.

The phone rang twice before Mocha answered. "Montana?" Her voice was low, and weary. "We're here at the hotel." "I know. That's why I'm calling." He stood under a tree just outside the country club, one hand in his coat pocket, eyes scanning the empty parking lot. I hear that you have made contact with my friends in Toronto. Mocha smiled and all she could say "Montana's protection. He'd kept his promise, even from a continent away. Mocha confirmed Journee's suspicion and let her know that Montana had arrange for them to keep an eye on them.

The next morning Mocha awoke tired as she had not slept well. The anticipation of today's meeting weighs heavy on her mind. As well as the conversation she had with Journee as they spoke about their search for their birth mothers. Both Mocha and Journee showered, dressed, and headed downstairs for a bite to eat. While in the restaurant Mocha spotted Montana's men seating in a booth near the back. They nodded and continued to eat their breakfast. Not feeling hungry Mocha ordered a cup of ginger tea and a blueberry bagel and cream cheese. While Journee opted to partake in the continental breakfast.

As Mocha sat sipping her tea she began thinking about Jaxzon. He had not called nor text. And she understood why. He wanted to give her the necessary space. But deep down she missed talking and spending time with him. There was an undeniable connection between them. She knows that keeping him safe was her priority.

Mocha and Journee entered the private conference room. The room was extremely warm. Or maybe it was the tension prickling down Mocha's spine as Kingston rose to greet them. Kingston paced in front of a sleek presentation screen, his voice smooth as aged bourbon as he began laying out the business contract, media options, and international branding concepts. Journee sat with her arms crossed, eyes locked on him, scanning his every gesture. Mocha, seated beside her, had grown tired of the pitch. She was here for truth—not a marketing deal.

Midway through his presentation, Mocha interrupted. "Why me, Kingston? Out of all the companies, ... why did *you* choose my company?"

Kingston tilted his head. "Because you are the best out of the hundreds of proposals we received. You are Raw. Unapologetic. And because, believe it or not... I know what it means to search for identity when the world tries to erase you."

"But do you know what it means to be followed?" she asked sharply. "To have your trauma weaponized. To not know if the man seating across from you might have a hidden agenda working for someone else?"

Kingston confused blinked—once, slowly. I do not know what you are talking about. "I'm here because of your innovative approach in the tech sector and you check all of the boxes."

Mocha gut twisted. Because behind his smooth baritone and manicured image, she saw the flicker of something... calculated. A glance too long. A smirk too timed. Journee leaned forward. "I've done my homework, Mr. McIntosh, they do not call me a skilled surgeon in the courtroom for no reason. I am good at what I do.

We are aware that the company is going through a merger, and your board members are looking at closing several locations and filing bankruptcy due to improper management of monies. The room falls to an eerie silence. Kingston McIntosh, who was growing visibly uncomfortable under the weight of their pointed questions. The air was thin with polite hostility—Mocha's tone diplomatic but firm, her eyes sharp, and Journee's posture unreadable but alert.

Kingston reached for his water glass, “I assure you both,” he said smoothly, “there are no layoffs, no misuse of funds, and no merger that would jeopardize this opportunity. The media does what it does—rumors become headlines before the ink dries on any actual report.”

Mocha exchanged a skeptical glance with Journee. “That’s a lot of smoke for no fire, Kingston.”

He offered a composed smile, walking toward the bar cart in the corner. “In this world, perception *is* currency. But I understand the importance of transparency—especially when you’re deciding whether to lend your money, your name, your *truth*.”

Journee folded her arms. “And Douglas and Reynolds Technology is just as solid as you claim?”

Kingston nodded confidently. “Absolutely. In fact,”

As if on cue, the glass doors at the back of the conference room opened.

In walked a poised and elegant couple, both dressed in striking navy and silver business attire. Kingston stepped forward. “Ladies, meet Lloyd Reynolds and Laura Douglas, the co-CEOs of Douglas and Reynolds Technology. They flew in to personally confirm the company’s current financial health and clarify any lingering misunderstandings.”

Laura extended a warm hand to Mocha. “We’ve read about your work, and we’re honored Radiant is partnering with us as a platform to elevate your message.”

Lloyd added, “We pride ourselves on ethical development, sustainability, and investing in the future of companies that matter.”

Kingston gestured to the seats. “Please—share where the company stands.”

Lloyd and Laura took their places at the table and opened a polished presentation folder.

Laura began, "As of Q2, Douglas and Reynolds Technology has experienced a 7% growth in clean tech expansion, and our media investments are within forecasted projections. There are no layoffs, and our team continues to grow. The claims circulating online are from a known disinformation blog—ironically funded by competitors in the AI space."

Lloyd nodded. "Douglas and Reynolds stands on transparency. We've had annual audits with zero flags for five consecutive years. Our compliance history is clean."

Journee studied their faces, her attorney instincts on edge. "So, the rumors about Red Birch Holdings?"

Laura shook her head. "Red Birch is a shell Kingston uses for creative control. It's not owned or funded by Douglas and Reynolds."

Kingston leaned back in his chair, a proud but humble grin on his face. "There you have it. From the top."

Mocha remained quiet, processing.

Everything sounded perfect.

Too perfect.

Later That Evening – Kingston's Private Suite

The mask dropped the moment the door closed behind the "CEOs."

Kingston raised a glass and chuckled. "Brilliant performance, as always."

Laura Douglas—real name Charlene Yates, a theater veteran—smirked. "It helps when your script is this tight. I still can't believe you wrote that financial report from scratch."

Lloyd Reynolds—real name Marcus Gaines, former hedge fund pitchman—nodded. "You owe me dinner in Manhattan for this one. My 'Q2 growth projection' was pulled straight from BMW's 2019 playbook."

Kingston handed them both envelopes. "Payment as agreed. Discretion included."

Charlene flipped through the stack of cash. "And what about your muse? Mocha? You think she bought it?"

"She's skeptical," Kingston admitted. "But this bought me time. Time to clean the real books and keep the investors at bay. As long as *she* believes in the mission, the others will follow."

Marcus frowned. "And if she doesn't?"

Kingston's eyes darkened. "Then I burn it down before they get the matches."

That Night

The walls were made of glass, but Kingston felt cornered.

He poured himself a neat scotch and sat on the edge of the sleek leather couch. His phone buzzed in his hand.

He hesitated—then dialed.

The line clicked after two rings. The voice on the other end was cool. Genderless in tone, sharp in cadence.

"Did you meet with her?"

Kingston stared into the skyline. "Yes. Mocha McBride She's smarter than I anticipated. Intuitive. She suspects something."

A pause.

"And what did you tell her?"

"Nothing," he said quickly. "But I think she's connected. I think she might be *her.*"

The voice exhaled slowly. "She can't know."

"She knows *enough.*"

Another pause. Then the voice spoke again—quieter this time. "What if she's the one they buried?"

Kingston's hands clenched.

"Then the truth doesn't just rewrite her story. It *burns down ours*."

Click.

The call ended.

And somewhere, on the other side of that line...

The real secret child of Aldric McBride stood in the dark, breathing heavily. Watching Mocha's name rise like a flame.

CHAPTER 25

BURIED NAMES, LIVING SECRETS

Montana leaned over the table; eyes locked on the worn manila file Sarah had just handed him. “This is everything you found on *Bettie Jo Engle*?” Sarah nodded. “Birth records, juvenile court proceedings, old CPS transcripts, and a sealed deposition from the summer of 1999 that was never formally submitted into evidence. “Sealed by whom?” Montana asked, already suspecting the answer. Savion’s eyes darkened as he tapped the final page. “*Judge Aldric McBride.*” Montana whistled low. “Now that’s a name I’ve heard too often lately. “He’s like smoke,” Sarah said. “Always around. Never traceable.

***

The small white house was tucked behind an overgrown magnolia tree. Montana parked out front, boots crunching on the gravel as he approached the porch. The door creaked open before he knocked. Bettie Jo Engle stood in the frame. She didn’t invite him in with words, just a nod.

Inside, the house smelled of sage and old memories. "I figured someone would come around eventually," Bettie Jo sat in her old rocker, the creak of its rhythm comforting in a way only ghosts could understand. Montana sat across from her, recorder on the table between them, the air thick with the weight of the truth she was finally ready to tell. Mrs. Engle. I just want the truth. About your children. About the charges. And about the baby no one ever claimed."

"I was twenty-six when the court sentenced me," she began, her voice slow but strong. "Neglect, endangerment, and what they called 'willful abandonment' of minors. I was guilty of being scared. Guilty of surviving in silence. But I never abandoned my boys. And certainly not the baby I was carrying."

"My husband was a monster," she said plainly. "Backhanded me for breathing too loud. Had several girlfriends in town. Beat my son so bad once he couldn't walk for a week. And I... I was too scared to leave."

Montana leaned forward. "Tell me about the order to leave the state."

"They gave me a choice," Bettie said bitterly. "Do your probation in another state quietly or we lock you up. Said my presence was 'a disruption to the stability of the children's foster placement.' Translation? They didn't want me anywhere near the court's conscience."

"Where did you go?"

"Alabama," she whispered. "Lived with a cousin. Scrubbed floors and cleaned churches. Didn't make a sound. My probation was for ten years. But as soon as I was close to completing it more time was added for some erroneous violations. And as soon as I was free and clear, I came home to Maryland. Hoping I'd find a trace. A clue. Something."

Montana nodded slowly. "And the baby? Bettie Jo went quiet. Her fingers clutched the fabric of her dress. Her breath trembled. "She wasn't supposed to happen," she said. "But God doesn't ask permission when He writes a story."

Montana's voice softened. "Who was her father, Bettie?" Her eyes glistened, but she did not look away. *"Aldric McBride."* The room went silent.

Bettie looked down at her hands. "He was my husband's childhood friend. Used to visit the house when we lived in Ohio. Said he was doing outreach pro bono work for troubled families. But he had a way of looking at me... like he saw past the bruises, past the dirt, past the silence. I was drowning. And he threw me a rope, but it was made of thorns." Montana said nothing, letting her words unfold.

When we moved to Maryland our home life had improved. Curtis got a better paying job, and he agreed to go to marriage counseling. I found a part-time job at a retirement facility and soon afterwards I became a foster parent. We had been in Maryland right at two years when the abuse started. On this particular day Aldric had come by to see Curtis who was not at home, and he noticed that I had been crying and had some bruises on my face and neck.

"He told me he could help get the kids removed safely. Said he had connections as a judge, to social workers. Promised he'd make sure the boys weren't sent to group homes. But when it was time for court, he turned his back. Said he never knew me. Said I was unfit. And he made sure my baby—our babies—was erased from every system."

She met Montana's eyes again. "That baby was taken the moment she was born. No name. No birth certificate with mine on it. I only know she survived because I felt her. And because he made sure she disappeared in silence."

Montana's throat tightened. "Do you think he placed her with someone he knew?" "I think he had her buried in the system," Bettie said. "Changed her name. Maybe adopted out under another identity. Maybe kept tabs. Maybe... not."

Montana scribbled her last line in his notebook with heavy hands.

“He’s the reason you lost everything.” Yes, Bettie nodded. “He promised to be my salvation. But he was just a cleaner. The kind who wipes away women like me, so his robe stayed white.” I was a good mother to my children. I know I had to do something to protect them and those who the state placed in my care. The allegation of abuse was true but not inflicted by my hands.

Once inside his car Montana immediately replayed the conversation between he and Bettie Jo and something did not add up. Bettie Jo was not telling him something.

CHAPTER 26

THE WOMAN WITH THE FOLDER

The building smelled like old paper and coffee that had been reheated one too many times. Fluorescent lights flickered above, casting a sterile glow over a place that had held secrets in manila folders for far too long. Maxwell and Jerrod sat side by side in a narrow office with mismatched chairs and a single window overlooking an alley.

The door opened slowly, and in walked *Ms. Rena Whitaker*—the caseworker who had overseen their files nearly three decades ago. She was older now, her once jet-black hair a dignified gray, her eyes still sharp but soft with recognition.

"You look just like your mother," she said quietly, eyes falling on Jerrod. Then to Maxwell: "And you... you had her fire." Maxwell nodded once. "We need to know the truth. All of it."

Ms. Whitaker sat down, placing a thick folder between them. Her hands trembled slightly as she opened it "I've carried guilt for years," she began. "There were decisions made back then that I didn't agree with. But Judge McBride had power. Influence. And your mother, *Bettie Jo Engle*, was painted in the worst light possible." Jerrod's jaw tightened. "Was she pregnant when we were taken?" Ms. Whitaker nodded. "Yes. She didn't know it at first.

The night you were removed, she went to a church for help. By the time she returned, it was too late. The police were already involved." She turned a page. "She was convicted of endangerment and placed on probation—*but under a relocation mandate.* She was forced to leave Maryland entirely, under the condition that she would not contact either of you." Maxwell leaned in. "Why?"

"Judge McBride said it was in the children's best interest. That contact would confuse your progress in care. But in reality..." She looked up at them. "It was punishment. And control. Jerrod swallowed hard. "What about the baby?"

Ms. Whitaker hesitated. "The pregnancy was noted in the system. But the birth? That's where it gets murky. I never saw a birth certificate. Only a hospital log showing "*A female child was delivered prematurely and removed under court supervision.*"

Maxwell's breath caught. "Removed to where?"

"No formal records. No name assigned. That part... went dark. And McBride had the authority to seal it." She turned one more page.

"Your mother wrote letters. Hundreds. Most never sent. But one... she mailed to a cousin in Maryland. In it, she said something that stayed with me for years."

Ms. Whitaker pulled out a photocopy of a handwritten note and read:

"I hope one day my boys will forgive me. I hope they find her. I know she's alive. I know he didn't kill her—he just made her invisible."

Jerrod's voice broke. "He...?" Ms. Whitaker nodded. *"Your father. Curtis Engle*. He vanished two months after your removal. Last seen near Dayton, Ohio but there were whispers he ended up in prison in Kentucky under another name. He was never seen again in family court."

Maxwell sat back, dazed. "So, he was just... gone?" "He abandoned all parental rights under pressure from McBride's office. The paper trail ends after that. He might be dead. Or he might be hiding." Ms. Whitaker closed the folder. "I don't know what you'll find at the end of this. But I know this—your mother didn't walk away. She was exiled."

Jerrod turned to his brother, voice low. "Max... what if that girl... the one Mom was forced to give up... what if that's the person who left the letter.

Maxwell's throat tightened. "Then we owe her more than the truth. We owe her the family she never got."

Later that night in the car the brothers sat quietly, the folder between them on the dashboard. Jerrod broke the silence. "You remember when we got separated... that last night in the foster home?" Maxwell nodded slowly. "You cried until you couldn't speak. Said we made a promise. No matter what."

Jerrod glanced over. "I think we just found the reason we were always meant to come back together." Maxwell looked straight ahead. And somewhere deep in his chest, under the rubble of grief and guilt, hope flickered for the first time. Maxwell nodded and the only person he could think of was Mocha. What were the chances that she was related to Judge McBride.

CHAPTER 27

THE KEEPER OF SECRETS

Trevor sat across from Dr. Veronica Sutton, dropping a worn manila folder on the table between them. "I didn't come to speculate," he said evenly. "I came for answers. About Lilliana Banks. About Samira Townsend. And about why *you*—a respected physician an advocate for children—helped erase Journee Arielle Banks from the system."

Veronica exhaled through her nose, as though she'd been waiting to breathe for years.

"Because" she said slowly, "I saw what Aldric McBride was capable of. And I knew the system would protect *him* before it ever protected them."

Trevor narrowed his gaze. "Start from the beginning."

She nodded once and leaned back, folding her hands in her lap.

"I met Samira first. She was brilliant, but troubled. Carried the kind of grief you could feel before she spoke. Her home life was... toxic. She shook her head bitterly. I learned later her uncle was Judge Aldric McBride. Everyone revered him. He paid for her school tuition. Called it charity." "But it was control. Possession. And he'd been abusing her since she was fifteen. When she got pregnant, she disappeared. Dropped out. No one heard from her."

Trevor leaned forward. "But you found her."

"I didn't," Veronica replied. "Lilliana did."

Her voice softened.

"Lilliana Banks came to me—broken, bleeding, terrified. Said someone she once trusted had turned into a nightmare. She was pregnant. Alone. On the run. I didn't know at first that the man she feared was the same one who had hurt Samira. But when I heard the name... everything locked into place."

Trevor nodded slowly. "You realized he'd done it again."

"Yes," Veronica said. "And this time, the child's life was on the line. So, I made a decision. I created an alias for Lilliana and Samira. I had contacts—people who owed me favors. We scrubbed their records, placed the babies—under a temporary ward of the state, and assigned emergency contacts that couldn't be traced. Ashley, my cousin, agreed to step in if anything went wrong."

She looked at Trevor with steel in her eyes.

"I didn't just help them hide. I helped them *survive*."

Trevor studied her closely. "But you let —your own child—be raised by Aldric."

Veronica flinched, the only visible crack in her composure.

"My child was born after I broke from Aldric. I was his legal wife for twelve years, but the moment I learned what he'd done—to *Samira*, to *Lilliana*—I left. I stayed quiet to protect him. To build a case. But he had friends in high places, and when I tried to report him..."

She trailed off, her mouth hardening.

"They buried it."

Trevor was quiet for a moment.

"You were married to him."

"Yes," she said, eyes narrowing. "Before I knew who he really was. Before I understood that his charm was a mask for cruelty. He controlled everything—the courtroom, the records, even the women in his life. And once I escaped, I devoted myself to helping others get free of men like him."

She looked down for the first time.

"I watched Lilliana vanish. I mourned Samira like she'd died. And I raised my child in the safest world I could build for him." Trevor tapped the file. "He is about to find out. All of it." "I know." "And Journee?"

"She deserves the truth," Veronica said quietly. "But that truth will cost her everything she thought she understood. That's why I stayed silent. Not out of shame—but to let her *live*. To let her become something beyond his legacy."

Trevor nodded, slowly standing. "She's going to need you now. "Veronica met his eyes. "Then I'll be there. For both of them. "As he turned to go, she called after him. "Trevor." He paused. "Don't let them carry this alone." He nodded once, firmly. "I won't." And with that, the door closed behind him.

Outside, the sky over Atlanta turned a darker shade of gray. A storm was coming. But so was the reckoning. His next meeting would be with Judge McBride.

CHAPTER 28

SINS OF A FATHER

The room was dim, lit only by the blue glow of four monitors arranged in a semicircle. Each screen showed a different feed: one outside a hotel in Toronto, another from a courthouse lobby in Georgia, another from a rural post office in Tennessee. The last... showed Maxwell and Jerrod, exiting a government records building with a folder in hand.

They watched in silence, the light flickering against the shadows of their angular face.

They didn't blink.

Didn't move.

Just watched.

"Finally," they whispered. "You're all waking up."

On the wall beside them, sketches and clippings covered every inch—like a shrine or a battlefield map. Pictures of old group homes, adoption records, sealed case numbers, even a printout of Mocha's emails and daily schedule.

Tacked above them all was a newspaper headline:

"*Mother Convicted of Neglect in Tragic Case*"

The air was thick with dust and silence, broken only by the heavy breathing as they rifled through a tattered storage trunk. Their flashlight beam swept across baby clothes, court transcripts, and bundles of yellowed letters—most of them unopened, most of them marked *Confidential – Destroy After Review.*

Then they found the folder.

Thick. Leather-bound. Marked only by the initials **A.M.** embossed in faded gold.

Their hand shook as they opened it. Inside, a notarized paternity test, dated 1994.

Child : Matthew S. Sutton
Mother : Veronica Inez Sutton-McBride
Father : Aldric McBride
Result : 99.8% probability of paternity

Their body went cold. They kept reading, flipping pages with trembling fingers.

Adriana M. Engle – DOB 7/7/2000
Mother : Bettie Jo Engle
Adoptive Guardian Transfer : Kingston McIntosh (via sealed agreement)
Status : Confidential Placement
Paternity : Unknown at time of birth – follow-up testing pending.

Then another test—dated years later, with McBride's signature buried in the corner.

Adriana M. Engle
Father: Aldric McBride – Confirmed.
Half-sibling of : Matthew S. Sutton

"*Morgan...*" he whispered.

She had been right under his nose. Hidden in plain sight. Rebranded, reborn—***Mocha***

They kept reading. The final paper made their blood run hot:

Last Will and Testament of Aldric Benjamin McBride

- Estate to be split among verified heirs.
- Names to be added pending final paternity confirmation.
- Beneficiaries: Matthew Sutton (trust #1), Adriana Engle (trust #2), Remaining heirs TBD.
- In absence of contest, estate to be managed by Kingston McIntosh.

There knuckles turned white around the edge of the document.

"She was going to get everything. Half of what should've been mine. The rest, going to children they never knew existed."

Six years earlier

The house had been quiet. They stood at the back of the property, staring at the soft light in the window. Alana's voice floated out—calm, affectionate—talking to Payton, tucking her in. They had watched Maxwell enter hours before. They had no idea.

Alana had recently confronted Maxwell with a DNA match she'd been investigating—one that linked him back to a high-profile judge in Ohio. She suspected it would explain Maxwell's placement, the sudden sealing of records, and the foster care redirection after Jerrod's removal.

They had seen her in court once, researching custody records. They saw the same last name on a file: McBride. And that was enough. That night, they entered the house through the kitchen, gas can in hand. No hesitation. No remorse. Just the thought:

If you uncover the lie, you die with it.

As the flames spread, they stood outside and whispered, "You took my name. You buried me. Now, I bury everything you love."

They knelt on the floor, files surrounding them like corpses. Aldric McBride had made pawns of all of them—burying secrets, controlling legacies, and splitting them like chess pieces..

"I didn't start this war," they whispered. "But I'll be the one to finish it."

They took out a fresh envelope, sealed it with wax, and wrote a single name on the front:

Mocha M. McBride

Inside:

- A photo of the will.
- A matchstick.
- A note that read:

We share blood. But not breath. Only one of us will survive the smoke.
—ASHES

CHAPTER 29

CROSSROADS

Montana lead led him to Charleston, South Carolina. He was parked in his SUV at the back of the parking lot that provided him a clear viewpoint of the exits to the building. The night carried the scent of manicured lawns and expensive cologne, an aroma that clung to places like this—exclusive clubs built on old money and older secrets. His hoodie was drawn low, his hands tapped a rhythm against the woodgrain of the steering wheel.

He'd been here for hours, waiting. Watching.

The country club's main doors had been a revolving parade of laughter and wealth—men with graying temples and silk ties, women in pearl earrings and diamonds that caught the light like sharp fragments of ice. They trickled out one by one, their polished voices fading into the night as luxury sedans drove away down the winding drive.

But Montana wasn't here for them.

He was here for Judge Aldric McBride.

He wasn't here to confront the judge—not yet.

He was here to see him, to watch him, to confirm the reality of what he'd uncovered. The man who held power like a weapon. The man who, according to whispers had made decisions that had ruined many lives. Montana's jaw tightened at the thought.

The parking lot was nearly deserted now, quiet except for the soft hum of a distant golf cart making its rounds. Montana shifted his weight, eyes trained on the side of the clubhouse where a rear door remained unguarded. And then he saw him.

Judge McBride emerged like a shadow himself, tall and commanding despite his age. His hair, silver and perfectly combed, gleamed beneath the dim lights. He wore a charcoal suit and carried himself with the rigid confidence of a man who had spent decades bending the law to his will. His pace was slow but deliberate as he headed toward a sleek black town car parked away from the main entrance, clearly meant to avoid attention.

Montana's pulse quickened.

The judge paused by his car, fishing a key fob from his coat pocket. That small, ordinary motion struck Montana with a wave of rage—the idea that this man, who had shattered lives with the stroke of a gavel, could enjoy such luxury and calm.

Montana clenched his fists, as he thought of how Mocha a woman who carried herself with elegance and warmth but bore the quiet ache of a lifelong question: *Where do I come from?*

Montana had found the answer. And it wasn't the kind of truth you deliver over coffee and gentle conversation. He thought of all the nights he'd spent piecing together this puzzle: foster care files sealed without explanation, records scrubbed clean, names erased. He thought of Samira Townsend, and Bettie Jo Engels and the way their life had unraveled like a frayed thread. And of the unnamed victims in this world unaware—or pretending not to be aware—of the devastation tied to the McBride name.

Judge Aldric McBride's sleek town car rolled out of the country club's parking lot. He started the engine without turning on the headlights, waiting until the judge's car was halfway down the long winding road before pulling out to follow.

The night was heavy and humid, and the faint mist of a late spring drizzle clung to the windshield. McBride's car glided through the streets like a shadow, weaving through Charleston's wealthiest neighborhoods. Montana stayed several cars back, his senses sharpened, his mind piecing together the puzzle he'd been working on for months.

McBride wasn't headed to the penthouse suite at the Parkview Resort.

The town car took a sharp turn into an underground garage of a high-rise downtown. Montana parked two streets over, pulling his hood over his head as he approached the building on foot. From the corner of the alley, he spotted the judge slipping out of the car, his posture sharp and alert, a leather briefcase in hand. He disappeared into a private elevator guarded by a security detail that clearly wasn't standard issue.

Montana noted the address. He'd come back. Walking back to his vehicle his phone buzzed and it was Sarah.

"Evening, Sarah," he said, closing the door as he entered the vehicle. I just had dinner with Trevor Rivers who is working a case that has ties to McBride.

"Rumors, mostly. Unconfirmed transfers of money to shell organizations, sealed court cases from the nineties that vanished without explanation, and... there's chatter about a woman who disappeared over thirty years ago after giving birth at the Haven Women's Shelter. You already know her name, don't you?" "Samira Townsend," Montana said softly. No, Lilliana Banks.

Montana knew that this was not good.

Sarah explained that Judge McBride had fathered her child. Montana was speechless not about McBride fathering another child but Trevor Rivers had been in contact with his ex-wife. Montana gasped and asked that Sarah set up a meeting with Trevor Rivers.

CHAPTER 30

BEHIND THE CURTAIN

Mocha stood at the window, arms crossed, eyes fixed on the glow of the skyline. Her reflection stared back, uncertain but determined. Journee sat at the table behind her, tapping on a tablet.

"I've rewatched that whole meeting," Journee said. "The way Kingston controlled the narrative... even his so-called 'CEOs'—too polished. Too scripted." Unbeknownst to Mocha, Journee had secretly taped their meeting with Kingston.

Mocha turned. "I felt that. Like it was choreographed."

Journee nodded, scrolling through business records. "That's because it *was.* I ran a reverse image search on Lloyd Reynolds and Laura Douglas. They're actors. Well-paid. Commercial work. Nothing to do with Reynolds and Douglas Technology."

Mocha blinked. "So the entire performance was fake?"

"Drama 101," Journee muttered. "Smoke and mirrors. Kingston wanted to buy time, or your loyalty—or both." Mocha grabbed her phone, and tossed it in frustration. "And I almost gave him a piece of my mind.." Exhausted from today's meeting Mocha showered and went to bed.

The Next Morning – *Toronto Central Library Archives Division*

disguised in sunglasses and knitted caps, Mocha and Journee entered quietly and found a quiet corner. Journee had called in a favor from a local journalist friend who provided access to the backdoor.

They searched through archived news reports, court bulletins, and corporate registrations tied to *Kingston McIntosh, Red Birch Holdings, and AshLight Projects.*

After two hours of cross-checking:

"Here." Journee pointed. "Red Birch Holdings was established in '91 as a private family trust. The primary financier? Judge Aldric McBride."

Mocha leaned in. "So this all starts with the judge".

"And twisted it into something new." Journee added, "AshLight Projects was launched using donation capital from a fund originally meant for *youth reunification programs.* Two years after Judge Aldric niece vanished from public record." Journee turned. "He used *her life* to build his empire."

Mocha froze.

What did you stay his name was Mocha asked. Both Journee and Mocha stared at one another. " McBride." Before she could get it out Journee replied do you think you are related to him? I am not sure. Montana only was able to provide me with my birth mother's name.

Mocha's eyes burned, but her voice remained steady. "We need to prove it. Before Kingston erases the trail." Mocha reached out to Montana and filled him in on what had happen at the meeting with Kingston, and what Journee had uncovered today. Montana listened without interruption as he text his contact in Toronto. *" I need eyes and intel on Kingston McIntosh and do not lose sight of Mocha and Journee."* His voice was low, deliberate. "You need to leave Canada. Now."

She blinked, startled. "What? Why?"

"Mocha," he interrupted, "listen to me. You and Journee need to be on a flight within the next six hours. Journee looked up, concern flickering across her face. Mocha put the phone on speaker. "Montana, what's going on?"

There was a pause and Mocha could hear in something rare – fear in Montana's voice. Mocha assured him that she a Journee would be returning home on Sunday.

Journee investigative instincts were in overdrive, her gut was telling her it was more there. Her phone vibrated. She glanced at the screen—*Call from Imani,* her closest friend and one of the most respected investigative journalists in Atlanta.

She swiped to answer. "Please tell me you have something," Journee whispered.

Imani's voice was calm but sharp. "I do. And it's worse than either of us thought."

Journee's breath caught. "Go on."

Imani continued, her tone shifting into the crisp cadence she used when delivering hard truths.

"The AshLightProject... it was named after a little girl. Ashley 'Ash' Newkirk. She disappeared when she was nine years old—vanished from her private school's playground in Bethesda. No ransom, no note, no suspects. The case was quietly closed six months later, labeled a kidnapping with 'insufficient evidence.' But here's the kicker: every single officer on that case was transferred, promoted, or paid off. It vanished from the headlines overnight."

Journee felt her heart pound against her ribs. "That's not all, is it?"

"No," Imani said gravely. "Two years after Ashley disappeared, Kingston McIntosh launched the AshLightProject—a so-called philanthropic research fund supposedly focused on youth advocacy and safety technology. But the AshProject is a shell. Millions funneled into it with no proof of field work, no deliverables, and an encrypted database only a handful of people could access."

Journee's fingers flew over her laptop, pulling up archived news clippings Imani sent over. A sweet-faced child with curly hair and a toothy smile stared back at her. *Ashley Newkirk.*

"This is why Kingston looked like he was sweating bullets when we asked about the funding sources. He's hiding something. Maybe Ashley's disappearance wasn't random."

Imani hesitated. "There's something else... something personal. You need to brace yourself."

CHAPTER 31

THE POWER OF THE HEART

Jaxzon leaned against the balcony railing of his penthouse suite, watching traffic stream beneath him. He held a glass of spring water in one hand, his phone in the other, thumb hovering over the call button.

He'd just returned from Germany, where he had spent the last several days with Dr. Lukas Weber, the climate scientist whose influence had shaped his passion for renewable technology. Their meeting at the Heidelberg Institute of Environmental Design had gone better than expected.

Dr. Weber, a stoic man with silver-streaked hair and glacier-blue eyes, had been captivated by Jaxzon's prototype a modular solar-energy converter designed to retrofit older city infrastructure without demolition.

"Your model," Weber had said, "isn't just efficient. It's *disruptive*. You've found a way to make solar energy scalable and retroactive. That's legacy thinking."

Jaxzon's inbox was flooded with requests from potential investors—European climate foundations, American clean-tech lobbyists, and even whispers from the Department of Energy. He should have felt triumphant. But his thoughts kept circling back to Mocha.

Jaxzon walked a few feet from the balcony and entered the spacious bedroom. He took a seat by the window, journal in his lap. The clouds outside looked like oceans suspended in the sky. He had scribbled her name again and again on the paper: Mocha.

Mocha

Mocha

He still wasn't sure what he was feeling. But he knew it was different. He thought of her laugh, her guarded gaze, the way her fingers curled when she was holding back the truth. And the look she gave him the last time they were together—uncertain, protective, but not indifferent.

They had shared something. But was it real? That was a question Mocha had asked of him when they last spoke. It had only been a short span of time that they had known one another and he understood her hesitation. Replaying the conversation he had with his mother echo loudly "Then be her water. Not to fix her... but to stay near the flame and not run." He knew that he was not a man who ran away at the first sign of trouble. He would give her the space she needed.

Jaxzon woke before dawn, the city still soft and quiet as he glanced outside his window. The inbox on his phone blinked with investor interest—messages about licensing, about rapid scaling, about who could be brought on to shepherd the prototype into production. The world wanted a piece of what he had built, loud and fast. He could feel the momentum like a physical force, an insistence to move, to close, to capitalize.

But his thoughts kept moving in a different direction: toward Mocha. His phone buzzed again and it was a text from Malika "*There is a gentleman that would like to speak with you and said it was urgent and you would know what he was referring too."*

Jaxzon did not text back but immediately dialed Malika's cell phone number.

Hi Jax. Is the man still in the office. Yes, Malika replied. Please put me on speaker. Doing as she was asked, Malika placed the call on speaker. Speaking in German Jaxzon said, *Lass das Paket bei meiner Sekretärin, und ich rufe dich später an.* The gentleman handed the sealed brown legal envelope to Malika and turned and walked out of the office. Damn Jax Malika said as she locked the door to the office. I am afraid to asked what you said.. It felt as if I was in a scene from a James Bond movie Malika said as they both laughed.

Jaxzon arrived at the office at nine sharp, his usual calm but commanding presence filling the room. The morning sunlight caught the edge of the sealed brown envelope resting neatly on his desk, exactly where Malika had placed it.

"Good work," he said with a faint nod, acknowledging her without needing to ask for an update.

Malika folded her arms, curiosity etched across her face. "So... are you going to tell me what was in that little James Bond moment this morning?"

Jaxzon smirked, loosening the cuff of his tailored jacket before taking a seat. "Let's just say some people prefer discretion. That gentleman was a courier. The envelope—" he tapped it with his finger "—contains information that doesn't belong in digital form. Paper leaves less of a trail."

Malika raised a brow. "So you're working with spies now?"

"Not spies," Jaxzon corrected, his voice low and steady. "Partners. People who know things that can't be shared over a call or an email. What's inside here... will decide my next move."

He opened the envelope carefully, sliding out a thick set of documents bound with a black band. The top page was stamped *CONFIDENTIAL* in bold red letters.

Malika leaned forward, whispering as if the walls had ears. "And what exactly are we looking at?"

Jaxzon scanned the first few lines, his jaw tightening. "Financial records. Ownership transfers. And something about an offshore account tied to the McBride conglomerate." He paused, eyes narrowing. "This isn't just business—it's leverage. Someone's been moving money under the radar, and if I'm right, it connects to Mocha's family."

Malika gasped. "You mean this could explain why you've come into work with a grin on your face.?"

Jaxzon slid the documents back into the envelope and looked up, his expression unreadable. "Exactly. And until I can verify what's in here, no one else can know. Not yet."

Malika shivered, realizing she had stepped into a game much bigger than she had imagined.

Jaxzon stayed in his office long after Malika left, the sealed envelope reopened and spread across his desk like pieces of a dangerous puzzle. The numbers on the offshore accounts aligned too perfectly with the trail of shell companies that Edgar had been tracking for months. Whoever orchestrated this had power, reach, and the arrogance to think no one would notice.

He leaned back in his chair, rubbing his temples. For years, he had worked in and around law enforcement – not as a badge-wielding officer, but as an observer who could solve what others couldn't. His father, a decorated former federal agent, had groomed him to think like an investigator. "Follow the money, son. Paper doesn't lie, but people do," his father used to say.

That voice echoed in his mind, a reminder of the bond between them—and the secret Leland Jefferies had carried for too long.

Jaxzon believed his father left law enforcement because the politics had become unbearable. That was only part of the truth. The real reason? Leland had stumbled across corruption that reached higher than even he could imagine—names and faces his father trusted. If his father knew Jaxzon had been investigating men he once called brothers, it would break him.

So, he buried it. Quietly. Alone.

The investigation had cost him dearly, including his marriage.

On paper, the divorce was mutual—two people "growing apart." In reality, it was far more complicated. His mother, had been pulled into his secrets. She loved him, but she couldn't live in the shadows he inhabited, never knowing who was calling, watching, or threatening. The final straw came the night she discovered a burner phone hidden in their home, one Leland had never told her about. He had sworn it was for her safety, but to Claudia it was a sign that his loyalty was divided—between her and a life she wanted no part of.

He had let her go, not because he stopped loving her, but because he loved her too much to drag her deeper into his world.

Now, as he thumbed through the documents, he saw the same patterns that had once destroyed his parent's marriage. Offshore accounts tied to powerful families, quiet payments to silenced voices, and connections that pointed dangerously close to Mocha's bloodline.

His phone buzzed. It was a secure line. He answered. "Jax," a voice said, low and cautious. "We traced one of the accounts. It's not just money laundering. There's a federal agent attached. High-ranking."

Jaxzon's stomach dropped.

Not again.

The secret his father had buried for years was clawing its way back into the light.

CHAPTER 32

INTO DEEP

Montana had spoken with Sarah and confirmed that Trevor had agreed to meet with him at her office that Friday at six. With that confirmation, he drove toward the same hotel where he had followed Judge McBride two days earlier. He parked across the street; his gaze fixed on the lobby entrance through a pair of dark sunglasses.

To his surprise, the Judge emerged—not alone but accompanied by a striking woman. The woman was in her early thirties, dressed sharply in a tailored cream blazer and heels that clicked against the marble as they exited. Her long dark hair framed a face that seemed vaguely familiar to Montana, though he couldn't immediately place where he had seen her before. The way the woman leaned in close to the Judge, speaking with quiet confidence, caught Montana's attention.

They entered the back seat of a sleek black Land Rover that had been idling near the curb. The driver, a tall man in a gray suit, opened the door for them before circling back to the front. Montana started his car, keeping a few vehicles between them as he followed the SUV through the afternoon traffic.

The Land Rover made its way across the city before heading toward the waterfront district—an area known for its upscale restaurants and private clubs. Finally, the vehicle pulled into the discreet rear entrance of the Meridian Club, a members-only establishment frequented by judges, attorneys, and corporate executives.

Montana parked half a block away, keeping his eyes trained on the pair as they stepped out. The young woman slipped her hand into the crook of Judge McBride's arm as if they'd known each other far longer than a casual acquaintance would suggest. Something about their body language—too familiar, too comfortable—sent a chill down Montana's spine. He snapped a quick photo on his phone, zooming in on the woman's face, knowing he'd need to identify her before the night was over.

Montana zoomed in on the photo he had taken, studying the woman's face as she disappeared into the Meridian Club with Judge McBride. Something about her features tugged at Montana's memory. He called Sarah.

"Sarah, I need a quick favor," Montana said, keeping his voice low. "Run a facial search on a photo I'll send you. She's with Judge McBride at the Meridian Club. Looks mid to late thirties, sharp dresser, confident."

"Send it," Sarah replied without hesitation. "I'll have something within the hour."

Montana ended the call and remained in his car, watching the entrance through the reflection in his side mirror. His instincts told him that this meeting wasn't personal—it was strategic.

An hour later, his phone buzzed. Sarah's voice came through, tense but certain.

"You're not going to believe this. Her name is *Alyssa McIntosh*– the niece of real estate mogul Edward McIntosh. She's been working under the radar as an executive liaison for the McIntosh Foundation. And get this—she did a brief clerkship under Judge McBride three years ago."

Montana sat back, his pulse quickening. Edward McIntosh—the same man whose real estate dealings were under quiet investigation by Trevor's firm, the same man tied to a string of judicial "favors" that had gone untraced.

"So, she's not just a random associate," Montana muttered. "She's a bridge."

"More than that," Sarah added. "There's financial overlap between the Foundation and one of McBride's offshore accounts—hidden under a corporate shell registered in the Caymans. Alyssa's listed as a co-signatory on the disbursement documents."

Montana's mind raced. This changed everything. If Alyssa was acting as McIntosh's liaison, then McBride wasn't just protecting McIntosh—he was *collaborating* with him. And Trevor's investigation into McIntosh's land acquisitions had probably hit too close for comfort.

As the club doors opened, Montana saw McBride and Alyssa emerge again, both smiling as if sealing a deal. The Judge rested a hand briefly at the small of her back before she slid into the Land Rover once more. The gesture was polished, almost rehearsed, but Montana saw the deeper implication—it wasn't affection. It was *control.*

He snapped another picture. "Got you both," he whispered. "Now let's see how deep this runs."

Friday Night

Trevor Rivers arrived looking every bit the seasoned detective—rumpled blazer, weary eyes, a badge clipped to his belt like an afterthought. He shook Montana's hand with a firm grip and dropped into the chair across from Sarah.

“I hear you’re asking questions about McBride,” Trevor said, his voice low.

“I’m looking for answers,” Montana replied. “You got any?”

Trevor exchanged a look with Sarah before leaning forward. “I’ve been working a case for months—missing girls, trafficking rings, money that moves too quietly to be legal. Every lead I chase dies in a courtroom, buried under rulings signed by McBride himself. I thought it was coincidence. Now? I’m not so sure.”

Montana’s jaw tightened. “You think he’s involved?”

“I think he’s more than involved.” Trevor’s voice dropped to a whisper. “I think he’s running cover for someone powerful. And Lillian Banks?” He reached into his coat pocket and slid over a black-and-white photo. “She didn’t just disappear. She was *erased.* Her name doesn’t exist in any records past the shelter. And the person who signed off on her case file...” Trevor’s finger tapped the photo. “McBride.”

Montana studied the image. Lillian’s smile was faint, her eyes haunted even in the grainy snapshot.

“And Bettie Jo Engles?” Montana asked quietly.

Trevor exhaled. “Her name popped up in sealed records tied to McBride’s chambers. There’s a file labeled ‘Engles v. State’ from twenty-four years ago. No charges. No verdict. Just... sealed. I can’t get access to it, and believe me, I’ve tried.”

Sarah leaned forward, her expression grave. “Montana, whatever you’re chasing, it’s bigger than Mocha’s parentage. You’ve got two women connected to McBride, both erased in different ways, both with children swept into the system. If this gets out, it won’t just destroy his career. It could expose an entire network.”

Montana sat back, his pulse steady despite the weight of his words. He'd been chasing ghosts, but now those ghosts had names, faces, and threads that tied back to the same man.

"Then we keep digging," he said finally, his voice calm but firm.

Trevor's eyes narrowed. "Careful. This isn't a case you walk away from. People who dig too deep around McBride don't stay above ground for long."

Montana smirked faintly, though his gaze was ice. "I've been underground before. I'm not afraid of the dark."

He pocketed the file, stood, and tipped his hat in a gesture of quiet thanks. As he stepped out into the night, the drizzle had turned to steady rain, each drop whispering a warning he didn't intend to heed.

Montana McGee had unearthed enough to ruin lives. Now it was about connecting the final dots.

And all those dots led to Judge Aldric McBride.

The next day Montana and Trevor paid a visit to Veronica Sutton-McBride. "Thank you for agreeing to see us," Trevor said, his tone calm but firm. "We're hoping you can clarify a few things."

Veronica gestured to the sitting room. "If you've come this far, I assume you already know more than Aldric would ever want you to."

They followed her into a space of quiet luxury—cream-colored furniture, a grand piano, and thick drapes drawn tightly against the storm outside. Veronica sat in a wingback chair, her posture graceful but guarded.

"Let's get to it," Montana said, leaning against the mantle. "You knew Lilliana Banks. Or should I say Samira Townsend?"

Veronica flinched, a flash of guilt in her eyes. "Yes. I knew them both. But not in the way you think."

Trevor leaned forward. "You worked at Haven Women's Shelter."

"I did," Veronica admitted, folding her hands. "I was a student, volunteering part-time. Lilliana was just a girl... terrified, hiding. She didn't tell me who she was running from, but I knew she was in danger. Samira arrived shortly after—another young woman with nowhere to go. They became close, like sisters."

Montana's gaze was unyielding. "And the switch?"

Veronica took a deep breath, her voice trembling slightly. "I didn't know. Not at first. Lilliana disappeared after her baby was born. Samira left days later, and the paperwork... it was all so confusing. It wasn't until years later that my cousin Ashley came to me and said, 'You do know they switched names, right?'"

Trevor frowned. "Ashley?"

"She was working at the county clerk's office at the time," Veronica said, her eyes distant. "She recognized the falsified documents. Lilliana became Samira, Samira became Lilliana. They thought it would keep Lilliana safe."

"Safe from Aldric," Montana said flatly.

Veronica's expression darkened. "Yes. By then... I'd married him. I thought I knew him. I thought I could trust him. I had no idea the baby Lilliana and Samira were carrying was his. And by the time I learned the truth, it was too late. Lilliana had vanished. And Aldric's reach was stronger than I'd realized."

Trevor scribbled notes, his brows furrowed. "You said *them*. You knew about Bettie Jo Engles, too."

Veronica closed her eyes briefly, her composure cracking. "Bettie Jo was... different. She was poor, desperate, trapped in a marriage to a man who drank and beat her. Aldric was supposed to be their family friend, but he... he preyed on her vulnerability. She became pregnant."

Montana stiffened. "With a daughter?"

Veronica shook her head. "No. A son. Bettie Jo had a son by Aldric. He was taken from her the moment he was born. I don't even know where he went. The other children? Foster care. Scattered. It was all arranged quietly. I wasn't supposed to know, but Aldric didn't realize how much I watched him."

The weight of her words sank into the room like a stone thrown into still water. Trevor leaned back in his chair, stunned. Montana's face remained impassive, but his mind was already racing—another child, another McBride heir erased from existence.

"You're telling me," Trevor said slowly, "that Aldric McBride fathered a child with his own niece... and another with Bettie Jo Engles?"

Veronica's voice trembled, but she met Trevor's eyes. "Yes. And that's only the beginning of what he's done."

Montana paced the room, his hands in his pockets, his mind mapping the implications. "Why are you telling us this now?"

Veronica hesitated, then whispered, "Because I'm tired of being afraid. And because if you're asking these questions, you're closer to the truth than anyone has ever been. If you don't stop him, he'll bury you the same way he buried them."

The storm outside cracked with thunder, making Veronica flinch. Montana turned toward the window, his jaw tight.

"So we've got two missing women, switched identities, children fathered by a man who sits at the top of two major metropolitan judicial power structures, and an ex-wife who knows too much." He turned back to Veronica. "Mrs. McBride, you need to decide right now: are you a witness... or a target?"

Veronica's gaze hardened, a flicker of steel beneath her fear. "Both," she said softly.

Trevor closed his notebook. "Then we'd better move fast."

Montana glanced at Veronica one last time before heading for the door. He'd come looking for answers, but what he got was a map to a dynasty built on manipulation and ruin. The storm outside was only getting worse. And somewhere out there, the children Aldric McBride had scattered were still carrying his legacy of pain. And one of them was Mocha. Montana was waiting on Veronica to mentioned that Judge McBride also was connected to offshore accounts in the Cayman Islands. But she did not.

He had learned to trust his instincts. They had rarely failed him, especially when the truth hid behind the polite smiles of people with too much to lose. And in this case, his gut told him that Bettie Jo and Veronica were sitting on something monumental—something that could unravel everything about the McBride case and the string of events that had haunted them all for decades.

TO BE CONTINUED

PREVIEW OF THE DAY THE LIGHTS WENT OUT

Book 2

Finding Light After the Darkness

When the darkness lifted, it didn't bring peace it revealed everything that had been hidden.

In the wake of chaos, each survivor must face the shadows of their own truth. Mocha struggles to reconcile love with betrayal, while Jaxzon stands at the edge of redemption, caught between protecting those he loves and revealing secrets that could destroy them all. Journee begins to unravel the final threads of her mother's story, realizing that healing sometimes demands confronting what you'd rather forget.

Maxwell and Jerrod's search through old placement files exposes not only the lies that shaped their childhood but also the bloodlines that tie them to a legacy of corruption. Montana and Trevor's investigation pull them deeper into the tangled world Aldric McBride built–one where loyalty is a weapon, and silence has always been the cost of survival.

Veronica Sutton, Aldric's ex-wife, emerges from the shadows with her own story to tell–a woman once broken by his control, now determined to dismantle the empire that nearly destroyed her. Her knowledge could free them all... or set fire to what little peace remains.

But the most dangerous revelation comes from Kingston's past. The young man's hidden connection to Aldric McBride changes everything–challenging his identity, his loyalty, and the meaning of family itself.

Meanwhile, the truth about Curtis and Bettie Jo Engles surfaces–an account of a toxic and brutal relationship that left behind more than scars. Their choices ripple across generations, linking them to the very heart of the McBride legacy and the darkness everyone thought was buried.

Finding Light After the Darkness is a story of truth unmasked, love reclaimed, and the strength found in rebuilding what once was broken. Because sometimes, it isn't the darkness that defines us—but how fiercely we fight to find the light again.

ABOUT THE AUTHOR

Dr. Calenthia Yvette Miller is an award-winning author, visionary leader, and CEO of A'Lure Publishing, LLC, where storytelling meets purpose. Known to readers across the country as *The Book Doctor*, Dr. Miller has crafted powerful narratives that blend real emotion, resilience, and redemption. Her acclaimed works include the *UNMASK Series*, *Love Letter Chronicles*, and the highly anticipated *The Day the Lights Went Out: A Survival Story*.

Born from humble beginnings, Dr. Miller's journey has always been anchored in faith, determination, and an unshakable belief in the power of education. Her love for learning began early and evolved into a lifelong passion for helping others discover their voice—whether through words, healing, or acts of service.

Beyond her literary accomplishments, Dr. Miller's heart belongs to her family. She treasures her children, adores her granddaughter, and finds her greatest inspiration in the strength and love they bring to her life. Family is her grounding force—the constant reminder of why every story, every lesson, and every moment of grace matters.

But her path has not been without challenge. After experiencing a stroke, Dr. Miller's perspective shifted profoundly. The moment became a turning point—a call to prioritize health, embrace self-care, and listen to the body's quiet warnings before they become loud. She emerged from that experience more intentional about balance, more passionate about purpose, and more dedicated than ever to sharing her truth through her writing.

Today, Dr. Miller continues to inspire others to live authentically, rise from adversity, and recognize that healing—both physical and emotional—begins with honesty, love, and courage. Through her books, mentorship, and leadership, she reminds us all that even when the lights go out, the power to shine again still lives within us.

We'd love to hear your feedback. Please share your comments on Amazon, Barnes & Noble or your bookstore website.

Discover more books by Calenthia Yvette Miller at alurepublishing.net

Thank you,

Calenthia Yvette Miller

www.ingramcontent.com/pod-product-compliance
Lightning Source LLC
Chambersburg PA
CBHW061123100726
47911CB00013B/656

* 9 7 9 8 9 9 8 7 9 5 1 1 4 *